SA

SAVE HER HEART
By
KC Luck

20190523

Thank you for your interest in *Save Her Heart*. I sincerely hope you enjoy the story. It was a pleasure to write. If you find time, a review, or even better, a referral to another reader, is always appreciated.

Please enjoy!
KC

CHAPTER 1
SAL

Salishan Bransen drank. The liquid was Txewian whiskey. A harsh flavor from an equally harsh planet. She spent time there in the past, on that small rock, well known for its many cheap liquor distilleries and rocket fuel plants. Sometimes, Sal wondered if they didn't mix the two. Still, in the dive where she leaned on the bar, Sal knew the Txewian was as good as she was going to get. Swallowing the swill in one quick move, she slid the glass back toward the bartender, a 0406-servant series android who definitely knew better days.

"Hit me again," she said, and he quickly complied without comment. Even though the shot would be her third in less than five minutes, she had yet to feel the effect. Years as a space pirate traveling the 8th Galaxy made her tolerant to about anything—especially when it meant keeping up appearances. She was once an undercover agent from the Space Ranger Corps and drinking and killing were her only options for earning the pirate's trust. *Not to mention I did a whole lot worse,* she thought picking up the new glass to shoot it down, too. In the end, the four-year mission to find the pirate's hidden base was a success, but for Sal the cost was high. *And so, I am a knight without a king.* She drank the next shot and set the glass on the counter. "Again," she said.

While the bartender was finishing his pour, Sal heard the bar door open and looked over. Instinctively, she scanned for possible threats, but it was only a human woman in a trench coat over a red dress ducking in out of the constant rain found on the planet NuForks. Her blonde hair was stuck to her head and water dripped to the floor, and the mascara around her blue eyes ran down her pretty face. After a quick glance around the nearly empty room, the woman hurried to the counter and slipped onto a stool two down from where Sal stood. "Something warm, please," she said, and the servant android flashed its lights but did not move.

"Such as what?" he asked in a monotone voice. "It's not like this is a coffee shop."

Sal snorted a wry laugh. "Give her a whiskey," she said realizing maybe she was feeling the alcohol more than she thought. Normally, getting involved in any drama was the last thing she wanted. *Best slow down,* she told herself and set the current glass of brown liquid she held back on the bar.

"I don't drink whiskey," said the woman.

Sal shrugged. "Probably for the best. It's lousy here," she said and nodded to the bartender. "Make her a cosmo. Top shelf vodka. My treat."

"You don't have to do that," the woman said with a waver in her voice, and Sal looked at her more closely. What she first thought was the rain's effects on her makeup were possibly from tears instead. Knowing too much baggage for her liking when she saw it, Sal pulled a dozen galactic credits from the pocket of her tailored black leather jacket and tossed them on the bar. It was time to go.

"It's nothing. Only a drink," Sal finally said to the woman as she started to walk toward the exit. "Have a good night."

"Wait," the woman said. "Please stay a little longer. I don't want to..." The woman hesitated, and Sal saw her glance around the bar as if nervous someone would recognize her. Not sure what to make of it, Sal looked around as well. There were only a half dozen souls in the place. A few humans and a few more aliens sitting in booths far enough away to not be able to over-hear whatever the stranger was about to say.

"You don't want to what?" Sal asked already kicking herself mentally for letting the conversation go this far. After a moment, the woman looked into Sal's face. Sadness filled her blue eyes but there was also something else. *A little fear?* Sal thought. *What the hell is going on?*

Finally, the woman smiled in a transparent attempt to lighten the mood and nodded her head toward the empty bar stool beside her. "I don't want to drink alone," she said. "Keep me company?"

Sal raised an eyebrow. She knew a come-on when she heard one and considering the dive was not necessarily a lesbian bar, it felt a little out of place. Still, the woman was attractive, and Sal had absolutely no place to be at the moment. *Who am I kidding? I have no place to be at any moment*, she thought and stepped back to the bar to slide onto the stool beside the woman.

"I'm Jade," the woman offered.

Sal gave her a nod. "Sal," she said and picked her whiskey back up. Drinking it was probably a bad idea, and Sal knew it, but living dangerously was something of her modus operandi. The android returned with Jade's drink, and once he left, Sal held hers up in a mock toast. "To new acquaintances?" she asked and went to drink when she saw Jade studying her. The blue eyes roamed Sal's face. She seemed to be assessing her, and Sal grew uneasy with the notion there was going to be some sort of trouble on the horizon. She wasn't sure what kind, yet. Jade lifted her drink and clinked the glasses together with a smile.

"How about to new friends?" she asked. With a sigh of resignation, Sal nodded and tossed the whiskey back. *To new friends indeed*, she thought and put the empty glass on the counter. Glancing over, she noted Jade's drink was gone as well. "My turn to buy," the woman said and held up a hand to motion to the bartender. Sal looked at Jade and considered her options. The best one was to walk away right then and find a hotel to crash in. Alone. Of course, the other option was to stay and see what the woman had in mind. Just then, the throwback digital jukebox started up, and Sal watched a couple move out onto the bar's dance floor. It was a slow song, and before she knew what she was doing, Sal turned to Jade.

"Dance?" she asked. The woman looked caught off guard, and Sal immediately regretted her stupidly spontaneous offer. *What the hell has gotten into me?* she thought. Normally, Sal never said anything or made any move without carefully calculating it first. There was simply something about this particular woman. A familiar feel to her. *I need to get the hell out of here.* Sal held up a hand in apology. "Never mind," she said but was too late. Jade slid off her barstool. Slowly, she unbuttoned her trench coat and set it aside. Sal had to admit, the woman's graceful movement was sexy, and she wondered if Jade was aware of it. *She's beautiful, I'm half-drunk after all, and now we're going to dance. I am truly an idiot.*

"I'd like that," Jade said and offered her hand. Feeling obligated, Sal took it and led the woman to the small dance floor. At first, Sal planned to make the whole thing as chaste as possible, but it was immediately clear Jade had different ideas. She moved in close and slipped her arms around Sal's shoulders until their bodies were brushing. Sal felt heat bloom low in her stomach, faster and deeper than she would normally expect. *What in the hell is it with this woman?* she thought. Sal was usually in complete control of her body and all emotions, but Jade was turning her on with only a simple slow dance. It was not like Sal was without lovers since she went on the run six months before. In fact, she spent the first few weeks on a harem planet where for a few thousand credits, you could do whatever your mind could think up. Sal chalked the expense up to therapy. There was a woman named Catherine she was trying very hard to forget, and for the most part, it worked.

And here is Jade, she thought and slid her hands along the woman's hips to her back before pulling their bodies tightly together. The move invoked a gasp of surprised pleasure from her new partner, and Sal smiled. If this woman wanted to play with fire, she would give it to her. *What will it hurt?* As she started to dip her head to nuzzle the woman's hair, the music changed to a livelier tempo. Gritting her teeth at the lousy timing, Sal started to let go. Before she could step back, Jade whispered in her ear. "Let's get out of here." The woman's breath was hot velvet on Sal's skin, and more tingles of arousal spread over her body. As much as she didn't want to admit it, there was something incredibly alluring about Jade. She could see no reason not to go find out more.

"Your place or mine?" Sal murmured, and Jade actually gave a quiet laugh. Without an answer, Jade turned away to grab her coat and slip it on. Then, with a flirtatious glance over her shoulder, started for the exit. Sal watched her and for the briefest of moments, wondered if perhaps she was making a mistake. She knew nothing about this woman. *Don't over-think it*, Sal decided with a shake of her head. She threw a few more credits on the counter before following Jade outside. It was true, Jade was a complete stranger and perhaps had a hidden agenda. *But then, don't we all?*

CHAPTER 2
JADE

Jade Hamilton did not expect to feel such a strong response to the woman. When she saw her at the counter of the dive bar, the physical attraction was instantaneous. Tall, dark looks, short hair, muscular. Everything she found sexy in a partner. But it was the charisma she was not ready for when she sat on the stool. Even the offhand remark to serve her a whiskey was somehow sexy. Perhaps it was the extreme confidence the woman put off, or maybe the touch of danger in her eyes. It all added up to take her breath away, which was the last thing Jade wanted. There was business to conduct, and Jade had every intention of getting what she needed.

The request to dance was also a surprise, and she hesitated. Her body responded yes, while her mind warned her to say no. By hesitating, the woman almost got away, but Jade recovered quickly, as was her style. Before she knew it, they were on the dance floor wrapped in each other's arms. She could have kept things simple and probably should have, but the chemistry between them was so intense it seemed to charge the air around them. She felt unable to resist. Moving in closer, Jade felt a flutter of arousal all through her when their bodies touched. Only the change in music brought Jade to her senses, and now, as she led the woman out of the bar, she was grateful for it. Her plan did not include lusting after this woman.

As they entered the dark street outside, the perpetual rain fell. The planet was notorious for its constant precipitation and Jade would be glad when she left it behind. She lived on Untas and was here only temporarily, something she hoped to rectify in the very near future. *Starting now*, she thought and turned to the woman. *Sal*.

"So, where are we going?" Sal asked with a raised eyebrow. There was a look of amusement mixed with hunger in her eyes, and Jade felt heat bloom inside her. *How long has it been?* she wondered. *Since a woman looked at me that way?* She knew it was too long and was able to admit Sal was an extremely tempting prospect. Jade grit her teeth. That thinking was way outside what she was supposed to focus on just then. There were more important things on the line.

"This way," she said, taking Sal's hand and leading her deeper into the shadows. Looking up and down the street, and seeing they were alone, she bit her lip. Uncertain how to proceed, Sal seemed to sense her hesitation and started to step away.

"Maybe this is a bad idea," Sal said and moved to let go of Jade's hand.

Jade grasped it tighter. "Wait," she said and not knowing what else to do, she pulled Sal's body to hers. "Kiss me." She watched Sal's eyes narrow and thought for a moment the woman was about to reject her plea. A knot of anxiety curled in her stomach as she considered the ramifications of not being desirable enough.

As if seeing the anxiety on her face, Sal's lips curled into a half smile, and she leaned in. Their lips met, and the shock of heat Jade felt from Sal's mouth made her shiver. The woman did not hesitate and drove the kiss deeper taking Jade's mouth with such passion her knees felt weak. *I can't be feeling like this,* she thought almost desperately. *Not now.* Her body disobeyed her though, and with a fever she was not sure she ever felt before, returned the caress. Slipping her hands up Sal's strong arms, she wrapped them around the woman's shoulders to pull her closer. Their tongues collided and a moan escaped, although Jade was not sure which of them it came from, and a throb pulsed low in her body.

In response, Sal reached for the belt on the trench coat and began to unhook it. Jade pulled back enough to help her without breaking the kiss. Soon they were both scrabbling at the buttons, and for a fleeting moment, Jade wondered if they would have sex right there in the alley. *This is insane*, she thought. *What in the hell am I doing?* Finally coming to her senses, Jade put her hands on Sal's chest to push her back. The kiss broke, and they were both gasping. "What's wrong?" Sal asked in a husky voice, and all Jade could do was shake her head. *Everything is wrong.* Before she could think of an answer, there was the sound of footsteps on the street behind them.

"I guess you could say we are what's wrong," said a man's voice. Jade felt Sal's body tense, but the woman did not respond in any other way than to slightly turn her head and look over her shoulder.

"Move along," she said in a cool voice. "This is none of your concern." For a moment, Jade thought the intruders might obey, but then they chuckled and moved into her line of sight.

Both were large and dressed in black combat fatigues. One human and one Rotu alien. There was no doubt they both were some sort of law enforcement. Running her eyes down the closer of the two, she noticed a stun gun on one hip and a collapsed baton in his hand. Clearly, he meant business.

"I think you're wrong," the closest man said. "Now how about you turn around and raise your hands where I can see them."

Jade watched Sal's face and saw she was considering his request. Slowly, she twisted her neck side-to-side as if to loosen it for a fight. Jade looked into Sal's face.

"Don't make trouble," she pleaded but was too late. Sal sprung back to close the distance on the speaker, and before he could react, her right leg lashed out in a sidekick to hit him in the solar plexus. He did not stand a chance after that, and as he bent over to try to catch his breath, she kneed him in the side of the head with her left leg. It all happened so fast that Jade was stunned. She never saw anyone move so quickly. Ever. *Like a blur of motion*, she thought and apparently, the second man was just as caught off guard. Sal bore down on him before he could raise a weapon. Not sure what else to do, Jade rushed forward to try and stop the woman from hurting him, too. The last thing she wanted was two maimed agents on her hands.

"Sal, stop," she ordered, and the tone of her voice apparently caught Sal by surprise because she hesitated. The man, no doubt trained in hand-to-hand combat as well, recovered enough in that instance to snap out his black battle baton. He made a wicked slash at Sal's head, and Jade thought it was impossible for Sal to move out of the way in time. With reflexes that seemed to defy nature, Sal ducked, and the weapon whizzed over her head by a hair's breadth. Off balance from the mighty swing, the man stumbled, and Jade saw a smirk cross Sal's face as she took advantage of the opening to pummel her opponent with two quick punches followed by an elbow to his face.

As the man dropped, Jade looked on in wonder. The damage Sal inflicted was shocking yet only took a matter of seconds. The woman turned and looked at her.

"Are you okay?" she asked. Jade blinked. *Am I?* she wondered. Things most definitely were not going as she expected. As soon as she set eyes on the woman at the bar, Jade knew she was special. *Not only sexy and charismatic, but ...* She paused and tried to think of the right word to describe the woman. *Formidable?* A smile came to Jade's face as she nodded. Sal was everything she imagined she would be, and from there, it was nothing but a matter of strategy. Tilting her head as coyly as she could muster, Jade crooked a finger at Sal to lure her closer.

"I don't think I've ever been more turned on," Jade murmured as she moved toward the woman. Sal smiled, no doubt ready to pick up where they left off. Licking her lips, Jade slipped her hand into her trench coat pocket and took hold of the small device inside. She carried it as a very last resort, and as she noted the two downed agents out of her peripheral vision, Jade was thankful to have it. The plan to take Salishan Bransen peacefully was an epic fail. As Sal opened her arms to let her step into them, Jade lifted the taser and pressed it against Sal's side. The woman's eyes widened, and her jaw clenched, and for a fleeting second, Jade thought she might not succumb. *Where in the hell did this woman come from?* Jade wondered, and then Sal fell into an unconscious heap on the ground. Shaking her head with wonder, Jade pressed the button on the commlink on her wrist. Her base team responded immediately.

"Holy crap, we watched the whole thing," said Jade's second in command. "Are you all right?" Jade was not sure. Her body still tingled where Sal pressed up against her, and Jade knew her lips were swollen from the hard kiss. Glancing down at the woman, Jade realized there was more to this ex-Space Ranger than she knew from simply reading her file. "Boss?" the second in command's voice asked again. It broke Jade out of her thoughts, and she shook her head to clear the craziness.

"I'm fine," she said. "Get two vans over here pronto. One for Bransen and another to take Tucker and Damon to the hospital." She clipped off the commlink before the man could answer. It was time to stop screwing around and get down to work.

CHAPTER 3
SAL

With her wrists and ankles in magnetic shackles, Sal sat alone in the interrogation room. Although she could not be sure how long she was left there, time was irrelevant to her. Remaining motionless was easy. She figured they were watching with hidden cameras, perhaps seeing if she would crack under the monotony. There was no way it was going to happen. She knew hell-holes far worse and learned skills of survival no person should know. This was a cakewalk and Sal would wait them out. It was that simple.

Besides, the time gave her a chance to reflect on her mistake. *Duped by a woman*, she thought. *Albeit a sexy as hell blonde damsel in distress, but still.* Regardless, once she was out of this bind, she was going to kick herself in the ass for being so stupid. It was not even an original plan. Wag a sweet treat as bait and catch a fish. This time though, whoever held her caught a shark. She intended to show them their mistake when the opportunity presented itself, and she knew it would. It was all a matter of waiting.

There was good news, however. Sal was confident whoever captured her was not from the space pirates. *If it were them,*

I'd probably already be dead, she thought. *Or worse.* The clean room, the shine of the shackles, and the fact she was not being beaten smelled of Space Rangers. Space Rangers she could handle. They had rules to follow and laws to abide by, which gave them a disadvantage. Sal lived under no such limitations. *Although, that was not always the case.*

Trained as a Space Ranger in what felt like a lifetime ago, Sal excelled in the academy and quickly became known as one of the best cadets ever to attend. Upon graduation, she was recruited as an assassin, and with every kill, became more of a legend. She was one of the elite. Young and foolish, she embraced the virtue of the corps and reveled in her success. Her future within the Space Rangers seemed bright.

When she had been pulled aside to take on a special assignment, Sal had not balked. Serving the corps was her life. Honor ran through her blood. Even though the mission had required going deep undercover, to the point her family and friends thought she was dead, Sal agreed to become a secret agent. Her mission was simple. Infiltrate the space pirates and find their base of operation. She had allowed herself to be captured on a transport, while posing as a civilian. The officers in charge of the operation estimated it would take six months and then she would be back to her normal life, with even more decorations and accolades. Thinking back on it now, Sal restrained herself from barking a laugh. Months turned into years. Life as a slave captive was a hell beyond imagination. Everything in her world spun down to only survival. Any connection she had with her Space Ranger contact was severed out of risk of detection. Even to the Space Rangers, she was dead.

Eventually, Sal worked her way up the ranks and became a highly regarded space pirate herself, but it came at the expense of her honor and her virtue. Sal became a hardened outlaw, and even though the mission eventually was a success, for Sal, it was a bitter victory. The corps turned their back on her when she returned and wanted her to stand trial for her transgressions while undercover. Sal was not interested in defending herself and went into hiding. *But they caught me after all*, she thought. *All over a piece of ass.*

More minutes ticked past, but eventually, Sal heard footfalls on the tile outside the metal door to her room. Sal took in a deep breath, held it, and then slowly exhaled to relax. Whatever the strangers had in store for her, she was ready. *And if they are stupid enough to leave me an opening to attack or escape, all the better*, she thought. There was a chime, and then the door's lock clicked a moment before it whisked open. In walked two human men, both in battle dress uniform, but with no insignia to show what branch of the corps they represented. *Interesting.* They moved to flank her, smartly standing back enough to stay out of her peripheral vision. Neither said a word, and Sal did not bother to address them. They were underlings and most likely knew nothing.

Instead, she let her gaze wander to watch the entrance. The next person to walk in the room was no doubt the reason she was there. Even though her face was expressionless, and her eyes were cold as ice, she was curious. Someone went to a lot of trouble to track her down, which could not have been easy. Sal made a point of laying low.

After another minute, a portly man in a suit, a hint of green to his skin being the only indication he was a mix of human and Martian descent, strode into the room. He was all business and looked as if coming to see her was an inconvenience. Sal blinked once when she recognized him. Petrus Cunningham. The 8th Galaxy's Chief of Staff. Second in command to only the president. *What the hell does he want from me?* she wondered. Cunningham had all the galaxy's military resources at his fingertips. As wanted as Sal knew she was, someone as high up the food chain as Cunningham would have little interest in her situation. As if reading her mind, Cunningham stopped. He glanced at her shackled wrists intertwined with a sturdy metal hook on the table's surface. With a nod, as if satisfied she could not get free, he looked her in the eye. Sal continued to wait, poker face in place. They stared at each other for a minute, and the room remained silent.

Finally, Cunningham smirked. "They tell me you are as good as they come. A real badass Ranger back in your day. Is that true?"

"Unlock me, and I'll show you," Sal murmured. Cunningham chuckled with a shake of his head as if she said something funny, which Sal took as a good sign. Being underestimated was always her favorite. It made killing opponents so much easier.

"No. As fun as that might be to watch when my guards subdued you, I don't think I want to go that route yet," he said. "Instead, I want us to talk civilly." Sal said nothing. She was more than content to wait rather than speak. The man's smile slowly faded, and he put his hands in the pockets of his expensive slacks. "I see," he continued. "You're going to play it cool. That's fine. It makes no difference to me." He took a deep breath and paused as if reconsidering whatever he was there to say. Finally, he pursed his lips and nodded. "Okay, here's the deal. I need you to execute a final mission for the Space Rangers. In exchange, we will drop all charges."

The news piqued Sal's interest. Not only because it would get her out of hot water with the Space Rangers Corps, but because she knew the mission must be difficult and dangerous if they wanted her to do it. Slowly, she nodded.

"I see," she said. "Do I get to hear the details before I agree?"

Cunningham snorted a laugh. "I think we both know the answer to that question. It's strictly a need to know situation. If you agree, I send the two guards out, and we talk in private." He tilted his head. "With your word as a Ranger to behave yourself."

It was all Sal could do not to laugh. *My word as a Ranger?* she thought. *That hasn't been worth a damn in years.* Instead, she gave the Chief of Staff a small smile. "Of course," she said. "My word as a Ranger."

Cunningham narrowed his eyes as if analyzing her tone for any sarcasm. Apparently sensing none, he waved a hand at the guards. "You can go," he said. "And send in Hamilton. She might as well be in here." *She?* Sal wondered with a hint of curiosity as the agents behind her walked out of the room without a look back. As if reading Sal's eyes, Cunningham nodded. "Your handler," he added. "Other than me, she will be the only one who knows the details of your assignment." Sal remained passive. His statement did not warrant a comment, although what he said made sense. The 8th Galaxy's Chief of Staff was too busy to run an undercover operation, yet Sal would need a primary point of contact.

After a moment, the door opened and in walked a blonde woman in a tailored gray suit. The fit was perfect, and Sal would typically have run her eyes down the woman's body in appreciation. Instead, however, her look stayed steady on the new arrival's face. It was the woman from the bar. *Son of a bitch. She's my bait,* Sal thought. The beautiful, and sexy, Jade.

CHAPTER 4
JADE

J ade watched the smallest, almost imperceptible, flicker of surprise pass through Sal's dark eyes before they once again became impassive. As if dismissing her altogether, Sal refocused on Cunningham. "Let's hear the details," she said, and the Chief of Staff raised his eyebrows.

"That's it?" he asked. "Surely, you recognize Agent Hamilton. After all, she captured the mighty Salishan Bransen. Nothing to say to her?" Jade watched as Sal held Cunningham's gaze. Her face could be made of stone it was so devoid of expression.

"No," she said.

When it was clear after a minute the woman was not going to say anything else, the Chief of Staff shook his head. "Well, this should be fun to watch," he said. Jade saw he was entertained by the animosity already between the two women. His attitude was the last thing she needed.

"Perhaps we can move this along, sir?" Jade suggested with a bite to her tone. Cunningham glanced at her, no doubt hearing the lack of humor in her voice.

He nodded. "Fair enough," he said refocusing on Sal. "The mission is a simple extraction. Go in, save our guy, get out." Jade watched as Sal raised an eyebrow.

"Simple?" she asked.

Cunningham shrugged. "Okay, maybe simple is the wrong word," he corrected. "But nothing beyond your capabilities if you are as good as they say at this stuff."

Jade studied Sal as the woman considered the information. Everything about her was dark. Short black hair. Deep brown almond shaped eyes. Strong features. *Incredibly attractive*, Jade thought and frowned. *Not that something like that matters*. It was true, in the bar the night before, Jade felt the chemistry between them. Sal's charisma was almost palatable it was so strong. *But it was nothing besides an aspect of the mission. A necessary analysis on my part before we subdued our target.* There could be nothing but a strictly professional relationship going forward. She refocused and heard Cunningham telling Sal what would happen next.

"Hamilton will brief you on all the details. She will oversee your insertion and extraction. If you have any questions, she's the one to ask," he explained. "As for me, don't expect to see me again. I can't be associated with this. Got it?"

Jade watched Sal. Again, there was almost no discernable change in expression. She could tell Cunningham was finding it unsettling, and Jade realized Sal took some enjoyment from it. The Chief of Staff was good at his job, but he was also arrogant and power hungry. Seeing him put in his place a bit by Salishan Bransen was a welcome change. *She really is incredible.* For the first time, Jade started to think the rumors were true. The woman was one of a kind.

Finally, Sal nodded slowly. "Who is the target?" she asked.

Cunningham held up his hands and shook his head. "What part of only asking Hamilton questions did you miss?" he asked. "I am not saying anything else."

Sal stared at him, not unlike a snake at a mouse, and Jade saw Cunningham swallow hard. "You tell me," she said in a low voice. "Or no deal."

Cunningham's face flushed, but Jade already knew he would cave. They needed Sal, and clearly, she knew it. The mission was too critical to screw up.

"Fine," the chief of staff snapped. "President Franmiller. He's not on vacation." Cunningham glanced at Jade. She knew the details already, but she was not about to help the man off the hook. With a frown at her lack of assistance, he looked back at Sal. "He's been kidnapped by an alien terrorist faction. And obviously, we need him back without anyone knowing what happened."

Jade studied Sal. She was no doubt processing the information but made no move until another minute passed.

"Because the United Federation of Galaxies has a zero-terrorist negotiation policy," Sal stated at last. "By agreement, the president should be abandoned to his own devices rather than compromise with the alien faction."

Jade heard Cunningham let out a frustrated breath. "Glad to hear you figured that out," he said. "Now, if you don't mind, ladies, I am leaving." He started to go to the door, but then stopped in front of Jade fixing her with a glare. "I don't expect to hear from you until this is satisfactorily resolved. Clear?" he snapped. Jade did not appreciate his tone but was not about to let Sal know there was any animosity between them. The less Sal knew outside the facts of the mission, the better.

"Crystal," she replied, and with that, Cunningham banged on the door to be let out. In another second, he was gone.

Silence filled the room and slowly, Jade let her eyes wander back to where Sal sat. The woman watched her with an unreadable expression on her face. Jade lifted her chin and returned the stare. She was not going to let this ex-Ranger, ex-space pirate traitor put her off her stride. This was her mission. As if reading her mind, she watched Sal slowly smile. There was a look of pure predator in it, and Jade could not help but swallow hard in response. *I'm prey in this woman's eyes*, she thought and against her will, she felt the smallest tingle of excitement at the idea. Then, she shook her head. *What the hell?* Jade was a decorated agent and successfully led over a dozen top-secret, highly dangerous missions. Salishan Bransen was only a pawn. *It is time to start making sure she knows it.*

Jade stepped away from the door and went to sit across from Sal. The woman tracked her with her eyes but still said nothing. Once Jade sat, she took the tablet from under her arm and laid it on the table. "This contains the top-secret information you will need to review before 0600 hours tomorrow," she explained as she held Sal's gaze. "In order to stay inconspicuous, a private star freighter will be our means of transportation."

Finally, Sal tilted her head. "Our?" she asked. "I thought this was a solo mission."

Jade nodded, pleased to have a dialogue beginning between them. The mission would be a whole lot easier if they could have normal conversations. "You will be solo once you deploy to the target compound. I will stay nearby with a smaller starship deployed from the freighter and be your means of exit transport. Once you and the president are secured onboard, I will fly us to a larger space station in orbit around the planet." She watched as Sal narrowed her eyes.

"And I'm supposed to trust you won't leave me hanging once you have the president?" she asked. "Or turn me over to the Space Rangers once we rendezvous with the space station?"

Jade nodded. She understood Sal's concern. There was nothing other than Cunningham's, and in a way, Jade's word to ensure Sal received what was promised. *Oh, I will make sure those promises stick*, she thought knowing the success of this mission and its outcome mattered to her greatly. Professionally, and if she was honest, privately.

Again, it was as if Sal could read her thoughts and now wanted to test her. The woman held up her shackled wrists. "Let's start building our trust by you unlocking these," she suggested.

Jade hesitated. She had a key and could unlock Sal without calling a guard, yet she was not sure if she wanted Sal unhampered yet. Even though Jade was well-trained and highly skilled at hand-to-hand combat, she had not forgotten what Sal did to her two agents in the street. *Or how damn fast she moved*, she thought. Still, if they were going to have a working relationship, she could not have Sal chained up like a beast all the time.

Taking a deep breath, Jade took the keys from her pocket. "Fine," she said and reached out to take Sal's wrist. The moment her fingers grazed the other woman's skin, she felt a burn of desire all through her body. It was like the woman electrified her. *How can one person be so incredibly attractive?* Jade thought while she clenched her teeth and forced herself to ignore the sensation.

"Problem?" Sal asked, and the mocking tone in her voice was clear. *And she knows exactly what she is doing to me*, Jade thought. That had to stop and immediately. Moving with cold professionalism, Jade roughly grabbed Sal's wrist and held the fob to the lock until the shackle released. The instant the metal yielded, Sal surged forward and grabbed her by the collar of her jacket. In a flash, she yanked her hard down onto the table. The impact with the metal dazed Jade for a moment, and she hardly realized when Sal wrestled the key from her grasp. Before Jade even knew what happened, Sal was suddenly free of all restraints. As the woman stood, Jade recovered enough to put up a defense. She was too slow. In an instant, Jade was pushed up against the wall and pinned there by the larger woman's body.

"Who knows I'm here?" Sal hissed into Jade's ear. Jade struggled to dislodge herself, but Sal was too big and too strong. "Stop trying to get away from me," Sal added. "And answer the question." Jade clenched her jaw in frustration, but let her body relax. Fighting wouldn't free her but she knew of other ways. Sal succumbed to her charms once, and Jade was not opposed to using them again if necessary. Slowly, she lifted her face to Sal's and their lips were less than an inch apart. The heat between them was thick, and Jade was rewarded with a slight, but very clear, flicker of arousal in Sal's eyes. The woman growled. "Who knows?" she repeated not lessening the strength of her hold. Jade hesitated. Sal's whereabouts were classified. Only a select few had any knowledge of her arrest. All transmissions on the facts were coded. In effect, almost zero people knew they were holding Sal there.

"Virtually no one," she finally answered. "We are not even on security cameras. You're on your own, Salishan. Now get off of me." Sal's eyes narrowed as she looked into Jade's. The moment held, and the chemistry between them pulsed like a heartbeat. Jade was not sure if the woman was going to kiss her or snap her neck. Then, the slow smile returned to Sal's face.

"That's the way I like it," she said and with a chuckle, stepped back to let Jade go.

CHAPTER 5
SAL

"Our probe images of the compound illustrate a likely weakness is the rooftop of this building." Jade said pointing to the holographic map starting to explain for what Sal counted as the seventh time over the last forty-eight hours.

Having heard enough, she held up a hand to cut the woman off. "Stop," Sal said. "I see what you see. Don't waste my time going over it again." Jade stopped, and her blue eyes narrowed. Her look, which was nothing but perturbed since Sal got the jump on her two days before, grew even more irritated.

"Since we have nothing better to do, I think reviewing the specifics is far from a waste of your time," Jade snapped.

Sal agreed with her on one point. They had little else to do. After Sal was smuggled onto the space freighter and provided special quarters deep in the heart of the ship, she was bored nearly to death. Only Jade came and went, which was not horrible as the woman was definitely attractive, but aside from talking with her, entertainment was hard to find. Mainly because all Jade wanted to discuss was the mission. Her ice-cold façade was growing boring too. *Maybe it is time to see if I can make Agent Hamilton squirm and scream my name*, she thought. *The woman wants nothing to do with me aside from using me as a tool to get the president back.* The challenge of it suddenly had Sal's attention.

Jade noticed the change. "What?" she asked, and Sal grinned feeling pleased the agent was perceptive enough to sense danger when it appeared on the horizon. *And I can be extremely dangerous when I decide I want something*, Sal thought. Taking a woman was a task she was exceptionally skilled in, and Jade would be no different. Yet, as Sal started to shift in the chair where she sat preparing to make a move, she hesitated. For some strange reason, overwhelming Jade by force was not what she wanted. Sal frowned at the realization and did not like it. There was simply something about the woman that put her off her game. *Almost as if ...* Sal shook her head, unable to grasp the edge of whatever trait about Jade was bothering her.

Cursing under her breath, Sal relaxed in her chair again. This was ridiculous, and Sal wondered if she was losing her edge. Months ago, she went soft over a young woman while trying to disable the space pirates' defenses, and Jade was making her reconsider her intentions too. *What in the hell is wrong with me?* she thought. "You can go," Sal growled at Jade. "I know what I need to do. Get me onto the planet and let me work."

With a wave of her hand, Jade dismissed the holographic display. She continued to stare, only now there was a touch of concern in her look. It was the last thing Sal wanted to see.

"Sal, if you're not mentally fit—" Jade started.

Sal shot out of her chair to pace across the room. Enough was enough. "I assure you, I'm mentally fit. Simply bored out of my fucking mind," she spat. Although well-schooled in waiting in place for days if need be, in her heart, she was a creature of action. They could not get the mission started soon enough for her taste. All she wanted was to meet the objectives, get a free pass from the Rangers, and leave this woman behind. *Far behind*, she thought. *But until then, I need to find a way to blow off some steam.* She whirled around on Jade. "So, is your plan to keep me caged up like an animal until it's time to go?" she asked making sure her tone was cold as ice.

Angry color rose to Jade's cheeks at the accusation, and Sal was pleased to see she struck a nerve. The least the woman could do was let her go to the space freighter's exercise facility. It must have one if nothing else than to give the crew something to do. Regaining her composure, Sal watched Jade set her shoulders.

"What do you have in mind?" she asked.

For some reason, Sal's thoughts immediately turned from what she could do outside the room and what she might have in mind to do inside the room. *Like in that bed ten feet away*, she thought and then mentally slapped herself. She refused to get involved, even if only physically with that woman. *She's nothing but trouble.* Sal was willing to admit to herself she knew that from the very beginning, but for a moment was blinded by a set of beautiful blue eyes and a perfect body. *I won't get blinded again.*

Narrowing her eyes, she pinned Jade with a stare. "Exercise facility," she murmured. "I want to workout. Stay sharp."

Jade pondered the request for a moment before giving a nod. "That's reasonable," she answered. "But I want your word you will not try to escape."

It was all Sal could do not to laugh. There they were again asking for her word on something. Sal's honor was so corrupt by now, she had no problem giving her "word" on anything. "Fine," she said, telling the lie with complete ease. "You have my word." In her heart though, she knew if any opportunity to get away and find a ship to steal presented itself, she would be long gone. Deal or no deal.

JADE WAS SMART ENOUGH to walk behind Sal, and she gave her credit for it. Initially, she thought the woman was nothing more than a paper pusher who ran projects from afar. That she was used as a decoy to subdue Sal at the bar, she chalked up to the fact Jade was attractive. *Bait,* Sal thought over and over. *Nothing but a pretty face and a hot body.* Once Sal learned Jade was also a pilot and would be flying her in and out of the drop point, she gave her a tad more respect. Apparently, Jade knew a thing or two about prisoner security too. Another point in her favor. Deciding the time was right to test out her handler, Sal waited until they walked into the exercise facility. There were a handful of others in the room working out, but she ignored them and turned to Jade. It was time to test her. There was a section of the room laid out with mats which no one was using. Sal knew from her experience as a cadet they could be used to practice hand-to-hand combat. Sal paused as they came to it and looked over her shoulder. "Ever throw down?" she asked with a wicked grin.

Jade raised an eyebrow. "I've been trained, if that's what you mean," she answered with a twinkle in her eye.

Sal found the response very encouraging. Working out her tight muscles throwing this lovely lady onto her back was exactly what the doctor ordered. "Good," she said. "Then let's give this a try."

She turned to face Jade who was taking off her jacket and shoes. Sal followed suit and then waited to see what the woman would do next. She was not disappointed. Without warning or any word they were going to begin, Jade launched a high kick at Sal's head. It was fast and well executed, but all Sal did was slide back out of the way. *Not bad*, she thought. *And I love that she came after me in an ambush.* Maybe Jade was a woman after her own heart. Before she could think about it further, the smaller, but very motivated adversary, launched into a series of punches and kicks aimed to disable Sal. For a lot of people, the attack would have been overwhelming in its speed and ferocity, but Sal found the whole thing charming. She ducked away or blocked each blow until Jade panted from the exertion and looked extremely pissed off.

"Well, is that all you're going to do? Not fight back?" Jade breathed. Sal tilted her head and considered what the woman was asking. *Seriously? Does she really want that?* Sal wondered. *Well, I've never had a problem giving a woman what she wants.* After dropping Jade a wink, Sal ducked down and kicked out sweeping Jade's legs from under her in a blur of motion. As the woman started to topple, Sal twisted in place and caught her as she dropped. Suddenly they were in an embrace an inch above the mat. Sal's face was so close to Jade's, they were almost in a lover's kiss. Sal heard Jade gasp but was not sure if it was from surprise or something else.

"Is this more like you were thinking?" Sal murmured suddenly filled with the memory of the woman's hot mouth on hers only a few nights before. A glance into Jade's eyes and Sal saw an unmistakable hunger there. As much as the woman was trying to keep Sal at arm's length, her body was not cooperating. Suddenly, Sal needed to touch this woman everywhere, and she did not care for it. Needing anything from anyone was not to her liking.

Slowly, she stood while pulling Jade with her until they were both upright again on the mat. "I think I'll go put in some time on the heavy bag," Sal said letting go of the still flushed woman pressed against her. "I need to hit something."

CHAPTER 6
JADE

As Sal walked away to find something to challenge her, Jade was pissed off, but also aroused, which only made her more pissed off. No matter what Jade threw, Sal did nothing but toy with her. *And then subdued me in a second with a leg sweep I never saw coming,* she thought. It was a blur of motion. Still, Jade could respect that. The part where Sal held her tight against her body was what affected Jade the most.

They were face-to-face, bodies pressing into each other. The heat that radiated off Sal drove desire straight to Jade's soul. *And a few other places too*, she thought and could not deny the physical response her body held at that moment. *What is wrong with me?* None of that was part of the plan. Not to mention Jade was a professional. A decorated agent with a stellar track record. It was ludicrous for her even to consider sleeping with Sal and risking the ramifications. *So why can't I stop wanting to?*

Breathing heavily, both from exertion and from being in Sal's arms moments before, Jade considered following the woman across the room to give her a piece of her mind. There would be zero tolerance for any more inappropriate behavior.

Yes, that is precisely what I need to do, she thought and set her shoulders. Before she took a step, Sal was at the heavy bag and pulling off her shirt. Underneath was nothing but a sports bra. The combination of well-defined muscles crisscrossed with scars froze Jade in place. *This woman has been through hell.* Suddenly, Jade felt less passion and a twinge of sympathy. Instead of seeing Sal as only the enemy, she thought it might be time to remember she was also a victim. Jade read the woman's file a dozen times, and the report outlined the undercover mission Sal agreed to take on. The notes included the loss of contact with her and the eyewitness accounts from rescued slaves which clearly stated Sal became one of the worst of the space pirates. Yet, Jade realized, there might be extenuating circumstances she was not considering. *What price did she have to pay to survive at all?*

Suddenly, Jade wanted to take Sal aside and simply talk to the woman. Not about the mission, but about her as a person. She wanted to know what was behind the cold and calculated exterior that made up Salishan Bransen. Taking a step, Jade started to ask Sal to turn around and then the woman was in motion as she attacked the heavy bag. In awe, all Jade could do was stop and watch. The woman's movements were a fluid series of kicks and punches, each so quick, and perfectly executed, it was almost like Jade was watching a dance. *A dance where any of those strikes could probably kill a man*, she thought and bit her lip as Sal moved faster and faster through the motions of her exercise.

Slowly everyone in the room came to stand and watch Sal's incredible display of skill. The heavy bag shook where it hovered above the floor as the warrior executed a series of jump kicks, each one from a different angle, and with such precision, her feet barely touched the ground between movements. Then, just as suddenly as the attack began, Sal stopped and stood motionless. She stared at the bag as if it were a person she could not subdue. Her chest rose and fell with deep breaths. Jade saw a sheen of sweat on the woman's back, but otherwise, she seemed unaffected by what was an extremely physical workout.

After another pause, Sal turned and reached for her shirt. As she did, Jade heard one of the men in the crowd snort a laugh. "Well, that was sure fancy, but I don't figure all those tricky moves would do you much good in a real fight," he said. "Maybe you'd like to spar with a real man?" Sal did not even bother to give the speaker a look as she continued to get dressed. With her top back on, Sal glanced at Jade.

"Ready to go?" she asked, and Jade watched the man in the crowd. His face grew red, and she knew trouble was about to begin. *Damn it*, she thought. The last thing she wanted was a fight to report.

"Yes," she answered and moved to lead Sal out of the room. The man was having none of it.

"Like hell," he growled. "You can't leave. Unless you're chicken? Because you know you can't win a real fight." Jade watched Sal pause as if considering her options.

"You don't want to spar with me," she murmured.

The man grinned. "Oh, hell yeah I do. I won't mind pinning you to the mat," he said with a laugh and looked at the others around him. Some were nodding, but most were backing away. *Those are the smarter ones*, Jade thought and reached for Sal's arm to stop her from hurting the man. Sal held up her hand to stop Jade's reach.

"One moment," she said and turned slowly toward her heckler.

"Sal," Jade started. "Don't do it." Her warning went unacknowledged as Sal moved to stand a few feet from the man. The idiot grinned with amusement.

"That's more like it," he laughed. "I'll even let you have the first shot. Let's see something pretty." Jade closed her eyes and knew the encounter was going to end badly.

"You're sure?" Sal asked with a tilt of her head.

The man nodded. "Definitely," he answered. "I can take anything you dish—"

Before he finished speaking, Sal threw the most basic of front kicks straight into the man's groin. Her opponent let out a little squeak before he crumpled to the mat. Sal stood over him, her face devoid of expression.

"Pretty enough?" she asked, and the man vomited. With a shake of her head, Sal stepped away and came to stand beside Jade again. "Now I'm ready," she said, and Jade wisely escorted her out of the exercise facility.

They walked back to Sal's quarters in silence. Not until they reached the door, and Sal stood aside while Jade pulled out the keycard to activate the lock, did she pause. As always, Sal's face was stoic. Jade read nothing there. *Does she even have real emotions?* she wondered and tried to remember from when they were clenched together on the mat if there was anything in Sal's eyes. *Desire? Anger?* The woman was a mystery. Jade sighed and swiped the card to unlock the door. "Get some rest," she said. "Tomorrow we deploy and get this thing done."

Sal nodded and started to move past her without a word. Tired of the silent treatment, Jade shot out a barb. "That was a dirty move back there. Kicking him in the groin." Sal froze, and Jade immediately regretted her statement. She only said it to provoke a reaction, but now she was not sure what it might be. Slowly, Sal turned and looked her in the eye. The stare was so intense, Jade forced herself not to step back. *She's a badass, I get that, but she's also just a woman*, she told herself and stood her ground. The look held, and Jade was beginning to wonder what she should do next when Sal moved in a blur. Suddenly, the woman was pressing Jade against the wall, and they were face-to-face. Sal's mouth was less than an inch from Jade's, and she could feel the woman's hot breath on her lips. The sensation made Jade's heart beat faster, and she felt a flutter low on her body. The instant physical reaction she seemed unable to control around Sal was back, and she hated it. Almost.

Slowly, Sal grazed her lips across Jade's cheek, and she had to clench her teeth to keep from gasping the sensation was so erotic. Unable to help herself, she reached out and grasped Sal's shirt. One part of her wanted to push away, and another wanted to pull her in. *God damn it*, she thought. Before she could decide, Sal whispered in her ear. "I have no honor," Sal said. "Don't you ever forget it."

With that, she stepped back and disappeared into the room. Jade let out the breath she did not know she was holding and let the door close. If she went in after Sal, there was no way to know what would happen. Shaking her head to clear it, Jade wondered, not for the first time, how in the universe Sal was able to affect her so much after only a few days. *Oh, let's be serious*, she thought. *I wanted to have her hands on me in the first five minutes of sitting down next to her.* There was something about Salishan Bransen. Something dangerous. Something exciting.

CHAPTER 7
SAL

With the mission finally underway, and the space freighter long gone, Sal was more than ready to start. Standing in the small holding bay of a P-527 spaceship circling their target planet, Sal ran her hands over the jetpack as part of her final check before putting it on. It was state of the art technology with sleek lines and a black matte finish. *Exactly what I need to get in and out before the sun comes up*, she thought. Satisfied, she picked up the feather-light device and slipped the straps over her shoulders. As she cinched them tight, Jade called over the commlink already attached via the conduction headphone patch around Sal's ear. "Status?" she asked. "We are coming around for entry."

Sal shrugged her shoulders and rotated her arms to make sure she was not constricted and then reached for her helmet. It was black as well, with a tinted facemask, and matched the tactical black clothing she wore. *Nothing but a shadow in the night*, she thought before answering her pilot. "Set," she said. "Count me down."

"Roger. Ninety seconds to the drop point," Jade said. "And Sal, I suggest you grab ahold of the arm bars until I lower the ramp. This is going to be quick and dirty." Under the facemask of the helmet she donned, Sal grinned. She was well versed in quick and dirty. *Just the way I like it*, she thought and wrapped her hand around the metal handles fused to the inside of the hull. She barely grasped on when the ship pitched hard left and then right. Entry at such an accelerated rate was always bumpy.

They debated at length about the best way to insert Sal. Jade wanted to land well beyond any of the alien terrorist's radar stations and then let Sal travel over land to the compound. The idea was less than appetizing to Sal. Walking through the desert terrain of the JawBan region of planet Eva-hom was not her idea of a good time. Her preference was to blast so fast through the airspace the radar techs would not even have a chance to react before Jade passed. It would seem like a flyby, and no one would suspect anyone would deploy from a starship moving so fast. Which was what Jade repeatedly pointed out to Sal whenever she insisted they start the mission that way.

"Even with a jetpack, it would be suicide," Jade argued. "I'm not signing off on it."

Sal shrugged. "Then forget the whole thing," she said. "Because I sure as hell am not walking clear across the damn planet." They finally compromised with Sal deploying from the moving spaceship, but into a field a few miles away in case she was injured on the way down. Sal had no intention of letting herself be injured but agreeing stopped the debate.

"Sixty seconds," Jade reported. Her tone was matter-of-fact, and Sal appreciated the agent's focus. They did not say more than a few words to each other since the incident the night before. *Just as well*, Sal thought and patted her belt to makes sure her plasma gun was on one hip and her combat knife was on the other. Jade tried to convince her to take an automatic laser rifle, but Sal was not interested. For this mission stealth was key. There was even a silencer attached to the gun. Sneak in, sneak out with the president, then call for a ride from Jade. Sal liked to keep a plan simple. Thinking of it now, Sal frowned. Unfortunately, she had enough experience to know the simplest of plans could go sideways in a hurry on any given day. She hoped today would not be one of them.

"Thirty seconds," Jade said, and Sal felt the spaceship break into the smoother ride of the planet's atmosphere. If everything was calibrated right, they would be on a perfect trajectory to pass the compound to Sal's drop site. "Lowering the ramp." At the announcement, Sal twisted her neck side to side. This was it and taking a deep breath, Sal mentally focused. Wind whipped through the cargo hold of the spaceship, and Sal slid her feet to the open door. *Let's get this party started*, she thought and bent her knees to prepare to run forward and out. "Ten seconds," Jade reported, and Sal started the final countdown in her head. There was a pause over the commlink, and then Jade spoke in a gentler voice. "Be careful, Sal," she whispered.

"I'll be right back," Sal answered, and with that, she sprinted toward the exit jumping out into open space. Sal let her body relax into the fall and did not fight the pull of gravity. Instead, she put her arms to her sides and pointed her body in the opposite direction than she agreed to go. The drop zone was still to the west with the idea being her momentum and the jetpack would let her land a safe distance from the compound. All of which would be followed by a slow trek to the fence line. That was not Sal's idea of a good time. Her plan was a little different and thinking of how much it would piss off Jade made Sal smile under her helmet. Traveling east and dropping at an incredible rate to avoid drifting too far off her target, she counted off another ten seconds. When she got to zero, she fired the jetpack, tucked her legs under her, and arrested her fall. Slowly, the powerful rockets strapped to her back won against gravity, and she was in control of her movements. The timing was perfect as the lights of the wire-fenced compound were now in view, and everything was where she calculated they would be. A couple of dozen brick buildings lined one main drag of broken concrete. Even in the limited light, Sal saw it was falling apart from disrepair. *A shitty little rat's nest*, she thought.

Using the boosters on her jetpack to maneuver toward the top of the tallest building, Sal's commlink suddenly crackled to life. "Bransen!" Jade said, sounding as angry as Sal guessed she would be. "What in the hell are you doing?"

"Making a slight adjustment," Sal replied at the same time she noted the presence of a dark figure on the rooftop she was about to drop onto. *Crap*, she thought and knew it was unlikely the sound of her approach would go unnoticed.

"There is a reason we—" Jade started.

"Got to go," Sal said into the commlink as she pulled her silenced weapon from its holder to take aim. As her feet hit the roof, she made a running landing straight at whoever was turning in her direction. In an instant, Sal identified the stranger as an armed alien terrorist, and Sal fired off a single shot.

The figure was motionless on the ground before Sal even reached its side. Lifting the visor of her helmet, she looked into the ugly face of a Ferg alien. She knew the breed well from her time with the pirates. They came from an impoverished and desolate planet, not unlike the one she was on now. To survive, they often took work as mercenaries or other henchmen. Scum, in Sal's opinion and contemplated what to do with the creature now. Her plasma gun was set to stun on direct order from Jade. Something about starting an intergalactic incident if a bunch of bodies piled up. Sal could care less about such matters, but Jade was adamant.

Not wanting to waste any more time, Sal disabled the alien's weapon and then grabbed the scaly beast by the back of the jacket to drag him into the shadows at the edge of the roofline. Thankfully, the thing was alone and did not appear to have activated his commlink before Sal shot him. All was quiet, and as she moved to the edge of the roof, she looked down at the road a dozen stories below. There were a few beaten to crap land speeders parked and the burnt-out relic of an old hover-craft, but nothing moved in the predawn light. Sal turned and used the night vision scoping devices built into the helmet to scan the horizon in both directions. Again, all was quiet. Everything was in order. *Perfect*, she thought, ready to get the job done and get out.

"I'm inside the compound, one hostile neutralized, in route to the first checkpoint," she said into her commlink, not wasting time with formalities. Kneeling, she activated the digital map of the compound inside her helmet and studied the layout to ensure it was in alignment with her visual reconnaissance.

"Good," Jade replied with a decidedly unfriendly tone. "Are you going to stick to the rest of the plan? Or have I been wasting my breath for the last seventy-two hours?"

Sal let a small smile play over her lips. *Oh Jade,* she thought. *You have no idea. At least I haven't killed anything yet.*

CHAPTER 8
JADE

As she circled in a shallow orbit over the alien terrorist compound, Jade was never more furious in her life. She worked with agents in the past who improvised on missions as the situation warranted, but she never experienced an agent blatantly going against the predetermined plan. It was quite clear Sal Bransen was nearly impossible to work with, and Jade was happy she would soon be done. *How could anyone be so stubborn?* she wondered. *And so difficult, yet be one of the finest agents ever to have come through the Space Ranger Academy?*

Frustrated, she shook her head. When Jade went through the academy eight years after Sal, she heard in class after class that the woman was the benchmark to attain for all others who came after her. Her physical skills, particularly in hand-to-hand combat, were unmatched. Even the male cadets could not keep up with her in the obstacle courses or during harsh terrain trials. Some thought she was superhuman. *And then there are, of course, her abilities as a sniper and assassin*, Jade thought. Above it all though, what she found most surprising was the fact Sal seemed to live up to the hype. Of course, it helped that Sal was incredibly sexy, and Jade would be lying if she tried to pretend not to notice it. Even now, a curl of warmth tickled low in her body. Clearly, Sal used her off-the-charts charisma as an asset, and Jade was not immune. *All of which makes her extremely dangerous. And is all the more reason I need to get this mission over, once and for all.*

As she continued to orbit, Jade tried to refocus on something other than Sal's dark eyes and incredible body. Those were distractions which did not fit in with her objective when it came to Sal. Still, her thoughts wandered to what it must have been like for the woman to go so deep undercover that everyone thought she was dead. Even though a lot of the information on Sal was top-secret, Jade's clearance allowed her to read Sal's back story. Her dossier made no mention of any family, but Jade wondered if the woman had a girlfriend or someone special in her life when she decided to take the mission. Of course, the assignment was supposed to only be six months. *Surely Sal would have had someone in her life who meant something to her.* She wondered what happened if Sal did have a lost love. *Does Sal still think of her?* Jade frowned pondering this extra element about Sal. *If she did, there are possibilities there ...* She let the idea go and considered her situation. *It's not like I have someone special in my life.* It was true, Jade was never in love, and frankly, she found the whole thing overrated. There were lovers, of course, although not for a few years and even longer since she found the time to form any relationship. Jade subscribed to the Space Ranger model: if they wanted her to have a wife, they would have issued her one.

Refocusing on the mission at hand, Jade checked the clock on the dash of her starship and noted fifteen minutes passed since Sal deployed. It was time for a commlink check in. Activating a switch on the dash, Jade checked her frequency. "Base to Chaos, report," she said wondering again at Sal's choice of call sign. She knew the woman was assigned a different one when she graduated from the academy, but she refused to use it. "Just use Chaos," she said and left it at that.

At first, there was nothing but static, and Jade wondered, with a bit of panic, if Sal was going so rogue she was no longer cooperating with the mission at all. *She would not do that to me,* Jade thought, somehow knowing that even though the woman claimed she was without honor, she would not be so heartless as to screw her over entirely. *Am I so sure about that?* Jade wanted to think they built a special connection over the last few days, and it was part of the reason she put up with the ex-Rangers antics so far, but a part of her also wondered if Sal was playing her. Jade pressed the switch again and repeated her request for a report. "Base to Chaos, second request, report," she said. There was static, and now Jade was seriously starting to get worried. She considered dropping back into the planet's atmosphere to do a flyover of the compound knowing the ship's heat detection radar and Sal's specially marked spacesuit would show up as a different color on her holograph. As she started to check her coordinates before making a move, the commlink squawked to life.

"This is Chaos. I am approaching the target's last known location."

Jade blew out a sigh of relief, both because the woman was sticking to the mission but also because she had not vanished entirely. *Maybe I don't trust her as much as I thought?* Jade wondered.

"Any obstacles?" Jade asked over the commlink.

"No problem," Sal came right back. "I haven't even killed anyone, yet." Jade heard the woman chuckle over the comm-link. *How can someone be so charming and so infuriating at the same time?* she wondered. Resorting to keeping it professional even in light of Sal's jest, she pressed the switch again.

"Do we need to review your exit strategy?" she asked. It varied based on the condition of the president. They estab-lished rendezvous points at three locations, and she expected Sal to use one of them, however, considering she completely threw their entrance strategy out the window, she was not en-tirely confident about what might happen next. Hence the need to check in.

"I hear you, Base," Sal responded. "I will assess the situation and let you know."

Jade sighed with relief. It sounded like Sal was going to stick to the plan. "Excellent," Jade said. "I'll check in again in fifteen minutes if I don't hear from you sooner."

There was no response from Sal to let her know she heard the last transmission, but Jade was not worried. It seemed the woman's style. Everything was by her own rules, and Jade won-dered if it was always that way with Sal. Going back to her original thinking around Sal having anyone special in her life, Jade could not help but wonder what it might be like to be Sal's girl. Jade puffed out a frustrated breath. The line of think-ing was not constructive. She refused to let herself have any in-terest in Sal beyond their professional relationship. The chem-istry which sizzled between them in the bar a few days ago was nothing but an act. *And I know that is bullshit*, she thought. It might have been the plan, but the reality was Jade could not stop feeling attracted to Sal. The good news was, in another few hours, they would be rendezvousing with the spacecraft carrier assigned to pick them up. They would smuggle the president on board, and her working relationship with Sal would be over.

As Jade watched the time tick along, she checked all her instruments and was surprised when she glanced at the radar and noticed the sudden appearance of two small blips. Jade leaned closer and stared at the screen. There was supposed to be a restriction on the airspace around the planet. It was one of the things Petrus Cunningham did for her in support of the mission. He came up with some excuse, which Jade was not privy to, but apparently not everyone received the memo. Two small ships were approaching. Turning to her computer, she pulled up the HD screen to get a better look at the advancing spacecraft and was even more surprised when she realized they were two A0406 space fighter ships. Those were not necessarily long-range craft, which meant they could only have come from the carrier sent to pick them up. *Which does not make any sense*, Jade thought. *What in the hell is going on? Do they think I need an escort?* Not sure what to do next or who she would even contact to get confirmation about the two fighters, Jade leaned back in her seat and tried to think. One thing was clear though. They were making a beeline for the location of the compound where the Fergs were thought to be holding the president.

Do they know something I don't know? she thought. Hers was a top-secret mission, but now she worried wires had been crossed somehow. *Are they on a recovery mission as well?* There were too many questions, and Jade decided to drop back into the planet's atmosphere in case she needed to intercept them. As she took up the controls and prepared to make her descent, the commlink crackled to life. "Chaos to Base," she heard Sal say.

"Go ahead, Chaos," Jade replied with a sense of unease slowly creeping into her stomach. It hadn't been fifteen minutes, so the only reason Sal should be checking in is if she secured the target. *Or has a problem,* Jade thought. As if reading her mind, Sal answered.

"Base, we have a little problem."

"What kind of problem?" Jade asked, already knowing she did not want to hear the answer.

"Seems someone got here before us," Sal answered. "The target has already been executed." Jade's eyes widened as she processed the information. The president of the 8th Galaxy was dead, and their mission was a failure.

CHAPTER 9

SAL

Sal knew from the moment she landed on the rooftop of the first building something was up. Everything was going far too smoothly, and she knew from years of experience that was never how things went. It was true, even though she would never tell the woman to her face, Jade's plan was solid. Plus, they reviewed the damn thing at least a hundred times, but still, plans never went off as expected. *Never*, Sal thought. This one should have been the same. After landing on the roof and disabling the one Ferg guard, Sal navigated easily from rooftop to rooftop, jumping with the aid of her jetpack, making a stealth-like approach to the target building. At only two stories, it was shorter than the others, more resembling a palace residence, hence her not landing on it directly from the starship drop. As she approached, she realized this rooftop, as well as all of the other rooftops were unoccupied. No guards. *And that is what has me worried.* She frowned. *If I were holding such an essential member of the galaxy in my compound, I would have guards in every corner. So, where are they?* She faced a decision. Keep going, or abort.

Slipping to the side of the roof, she peeked over and into the courtyard below. Still no one. Sal frowned. *Could all these guys be asleep?* she wondered. It was coming up on dawn. *Maybe Ferg mercenaries are lazier than I thought.* Seeing no reason not to go down and check out the space, she stepped off and let the jetpack gently lower her. It made only the slightest whooshing noise, and unless someone was paying close attention, they could easily mistake the sound for the wind. All she needed to be concerned about was anyone watching out a window. Even dressed in all black, there was enough light in the sky to see her descent.

Touching down, she spun on her heels and surveyed the open space protected by eight-foot-high concrete walls topped with razor wire. Once again, she was surprised there were no Ferg mercenaries in attendance. *Yep*, she thought. *I have a problem.* Every instinct told her things were not right. Still, her curiosity was raised as to why she was sent to this godforsaken desert planet and put on this mission to rescue the president. If it was a trap, the setup was an elaborate one and made zero sense about why someone would lure her into it when she was already their captive.

Unable to help herself, she decided to move forward. Sticking to the edge of the courtyard, she slipped along without a sound to the French doors at the back of the building. After another glance around, Sal slipped a device from her belt and prepared to pick the lock and then paused. Knowing from experience it never hurt to give the handle a try, Sal found it open. Unfortunately, she was not at all surprised. It was only another sign the Fergs were welcoming her into what had to be a trap. *If these assholes think I am not ready for whatever they have in store, they are idiots.* Pulling her long combat knife from its sheath, she took a deep breath to prepare herself. The plasma gun was still on her other hip, but it could be clumsy and make too much noise. Sometimes a job simply needed a knife. Like the rest of her outfit, the blade was jet black, and she sharpened it herself. It could slice through about anything.

Taking a deep breath to prepare herself, she made a quick scan for any tripwire lasers, and then slipped inside. Using the map in her head of the two-story floor plan, she crossed the foyer to the stairs. The layout of the building was one more thing Jade insisted she memorize and recite back repeatedly. If nothing else, Sal was willing to admit the woman was thorough in her prep, and thankfully, so far her intelligence of the compound was reliable. *Not that I will ever admit it to her*, Sal thought as a wry grin crossed her face. She was having more fun with Jade than she would like to admit and the idea of spending a night or two with the sexy Space Ranger agent was growing on her. *But let's not get distracted.* There was work to do first.

Within seconds, she climbed the stairs and made it to the floor where the president was believed to be located. On their first ten-thousand-foot flyover during the night, the heat sensors on Jade's ship determined this room was where they were holding the president. It was a bonus to know alien terrorists were holding the man because their heat signatures were different. *Ferg reptilian-type blood thankfully shows colder*, she thought and paused as she reached the closed door. Twisting her head side-to-side to relax, she considered the best approach. So far, stealth was working, yet if armed guards filled the room, her knife would only go so far. *Time for some firepower.* She pulled her plasma gun, readying herself to kick the door in and take out whoever was guarding the man. *One, two, three!* She rushed to the door, slammed it open with one flying leap, and was ready for anything except for what she found. A man sat tied to a chair in the center of the room, and although she never met him in person, she knew his likeness from dozens of photographs. It was the president of the 8th Galaxy, and he was not looking so well. The man was dead. Shot to the head executioner style and from the amount of blood still spilling from the horrific wound, she knew the execution happened recently.

Sal lowered her weapons and shook her head. *You have got to be kidding me*, she thought. "Base, we have a little problem," she said.

Jade's voice immediately came back over the minuscule speaker in the helmet. "What kind of problem?" she asked, suspicion clear in her voice.

If I didn't know any better, I'd say that woman doesn't trust me, Sal thought with a chuckle. *Smart girl.* "Seems someone got here before us," Sal answered. "The target has already been executed." As she finished the statement, she heard footsteps running down the hall behind her. She turned in time to see four men burst through the door she just kicked in. They were not alien terrorists, but humans in combat gear, and for the first time, Sal knew she might have a real problem.

As the men spread out, Sal saw one raise his wrist and speak into a commlink. What Sal heard him yell over the frequency made her raise her eyebrows in surprise. *And I hate surprises,* she thought.

"We captured the assassin," the man said, and Sal knew then what the trap was. She was being framed.

"Oh, hell no," Sal muttered. "Not today." Switching her weapon from stun to kill, she shot the man talking to the commlink first and then immediately blasted the man beside him in the chest before diving behind the body of the president to use him as a shield. Before she could decide which of the other two assholes to kill next, her commlink crackled to life.

"Chaos, report," Jade ordered. "What do you mean 'not today'?"

"Not a good time," Sal responded watching with frustration as the two remaining attackers were smart enough to retreat to take cover in the hall.

"Damnit, Sal," Jade said over the commlink. "Report!" Sal ignored the request when she noticed one of the men was stupid enough to try and advance. Sal aimed over the dead president's shoulder.

"I suggest you reconsider, Ranger," Sal growled, and she saw her attacker hesitate, but then he fired a couple of shots before backing up again. The blasts slammed into the president's body, and Sal knew her shield would soon be hamburger. *Not to mention these guys must have reinforcements coming*, she thought, irritated at letting her curiosity get her in this situation. She assessed the room and came to a quick conclusion. There was only one option, and it was going through the window directly behind her.

After firing off another round of shots in the direction of the doorway, Sal spun on the balls of her feet, fired into the glass, and watched it shatter in the same moment she sprinted toward it. Without a look back, she plunged through the opening while at the same time the rangers let go a volley of shots of their own. Sal felt them slam into her jetpack. *Now that could be a problem*, she thought knowing the current moment was not a good time for her ability to fly to be compromised. Engaging the thrusters to slow her fall, only one fired and sent her twisting in space. At any second, the thing was liable to send her slamming into the ground, so she shut off the device and dropped. She was only fifteen feet from the ground but still knew the landing was going to suck as her feet hit the ground. Rolling to absorb the impact, she slipped out of the jetpack, and sprang to her feet to sprint toward the alley between the two buildings across the street. Blasts landed all around her while she zigzagged over the road before ducking into a narrow space between two buildings and out of immediate danger. Talking into her commlink, she ignored all formality. "Jade," she said. "Sweetheart, I'm going to need a lift. Pronto."

"Do you have your jetpack?" Jade asked.

"That would be a negative," Sal replied as she continued to jog, reaching an alley, and checking both directions. "But I'm headed for the tallest building, and if you drop a cable as you do a low flyby, I will make sure I catch it."

There was a long pause. "You're not serious?" Jade asked.

Sal snorted a laugh. "Trust me," Sal said. "I am serious. And if you don't mind, get here in a hurry."

CHAPTER 10
JADE

This is craziness, Jade thought as she turned the spaceship into a nosedive toward the planet below. *How can the president of the 8th Galaxy be dead?* The alien terrorists were asking for ransom, so it was in their best interest to keep the man alive. Her intel was obviously wrong and being so caught off guard frustrated Jade.

As her ship plunged through the Evahom planet's atmosphere at an accelerated rate, she noted the heat sensors were flashing. *Coming in a little too hot*, she realized and activated the shields. Still, if Sal were in trouble, Jade would risk scorching the hull. As much as she hated to admit it, she knew if Sal needed her, she would risk everything. Checking her radar, Jade looked to see what the two A0406 fighter blips were up to at the moment. If the compound was where they were headed, she knew she would have a bigger problem. Thankfully, the craft seemed to have stopped to circle in orbit and were no longer coming in her direction. Their presence still puzzled her, but right now her priority was Sal. Her agent was in trouble and needed an evacuation immediately.

Flipping on the holographic map of the compound, she quickly picked up Sal's heat signature tracking device. She was on the move and almost to the building selected for evacuation. "Chaos, this is Base, copy?" Jade asked.

Sal came back immediately. "Copy. How about you tell me you are on your way," she said.

Jade detected the slightest hint of something other than cockiness in her voice. Nothing could have worried Jade more. "I am dropping toward your location now," Jade replied. "Advise on your situation. Can you reach any of the three original rendezvous points?"

"Yeah, no," Sal responded. "I'm entering the building where I need a pickup right now." There was a pause, and Jade heard the sound of a plasma gun shooting rapidly. "Luckily, these guys are stupid," Sal continued as if nothing exciting happened. "Going into the stairwell now preparing to exit off this roof in T-3 minutes."

Jade puffed out a frustrated breath, wondering how the original plan went so wrong. It was intended to be a stealth mission with an exit using the jetpack. She intended to get answers from Sal about how she screwed it all up the minute the woman was back on board. *Of course, getting her back on the ship will be the trick*, she thought. There was no way she believed Sal's exit plan would work. *Catching a moving cable? Seriously?*

On the map, Jade saw Sal's dot was reaching the rooftop. Other blips were coming up behind her and Jade knew she needed to get down there regardless of what happened next. Dropping lower, she prepared to execute a flyover of the compound and after another minute was able to make a visual of

Sal. Even as she steered the starship, with one eye still on the radar to monitor the fighters above, she could not help but be a little in awe of Sal's marksmanship as she fought off the relentless attack. In some ways, it almost looked like the woman was participating in a Space Ranger Academy shooting exercise where targets popped up one after another. Based on how accurate she was, Jade could only imagine what her scores must have been. *No doubt one of the reasons she was selected to be a sniper*, she thought for a moment before refocusing on her objective.

"Hello?" she heard Sal say over the commlink. "Things are getting a little ridiculous down here."

"Coming in hot," Jade answered. Although it went against any of Jade's logic, she saw no other possible solution to rescuing Sal. There was no time to land anywhere, and even if she could, Sal was trapped on the rooftop. "I have a visual on you, and I am coming in from the south."

"Well, it's about time," Sal shot back. "Drop that cable."

Jade was still not clear on the plan as it seemed humanly impossible for that to work. Even slowing down to barely above a hover while making her pass, her rate of speed would probably do nothing but knock Sal off the roof even if she was able to grab hold of the cable.

"Sal," Jade said. "This seems to have a small chance of probability of success. Don't you think—"

"Just drop the cable," Sal interrupted, her voice hardened to steel. "I am not dying on this rooftop today. Someone set me up, and I'm going to make them pay for it."

Jade shook her head, both at the stubbornness she heard in the woman's voice, but also at the idea someone sabotaged her mission. She agreed someone needed to be held accountable for the screwup, but it was only a misunderstanding. Just then though, with no other choice she could see, Jade pulled the lever to open the hatch on the bottom of the spaceship and released the hoist's tension to drop the thick nylon wrapped steel cable. It was intended for when the craft was hovering and allowed rangers to repel down. It was not meant to pick people up.

As she grew closer, Jade saw another batch of figures bulrush the doorway at the top of the stairwell, and she knew even Sal would be overwhelmed by the sheer numbers. *I won't reach her in time*, she thought. There was no alternative. It was risky, but Jade had to take a shot. "Get clear of the stairwell exit and prepare to duck," Jade ordered over the commlink without any pretense. "I'm going to fire."

"Wait, you're going to what?" she heard Sal say the moment she pulled the trigger on the laser cannon on the front of the starship. Her aim was perfect, and the top of the stairwell exploded. A ball of fire roared within a nanosecond of the impact. For a moment, Jade could not see as she raced through the smoke. She knew the cable was dangling down, but with it beneath her starship, she had no visibility to how close Sal might be to it. As she continued past the building, Jade held her breath and tried to tamp down the fear the plan would fail. Slapping the switch for the commlink, she could only pray the woman was still alive.

"Chaos, report," Jade ordered. There was no response. *Damnit Sal*, Jade thought, and a ball of fear formed in her chest. As difficult as Sal was to deal with, there was chemistry between them. Intense chemistry. *And I have other motivations*, she thought, knowing losing Sal would upset her on many levels. She could not help but care if the ex-Space Ranger had fallen to her death. Desperate now to reach her, Jade activated the commlink again. "Chaos, report," she said with a waiver in her voice. Again, there was nothing but static, and she considered turning back to do another flyover. *Maybe I can at least spot Sal's body.* In that instant, an alarm sounded on her radar, and she checked it to see the two A0406 fighter ships she noticed earlier were making a descent. *And they are* coming *straight toward me.* Because they were moving with such velocity, her intruder alarm was triggered and as she watched them close in, she considered the possibility she would need to take evasive maneuvers. Suddenly, Jade heard a voice on the commlink.

"Hoist," she heard Sal bark. "Hoist or lower me for God's sake." The order made her heart skip, she was so relieved. Knowing Sal was alive and secured to the ship, albeit precariously, helped her focus on the other problem. The fighters. Even though they were well past the compound, Jade could not slow down to lower Sal to the ground. She needed to do the opposite.

"Hang on, Sal," Jade said into the commlink. "I will bring you up, but it will be fast."

"Fast is good," Sal replied, and Jade could only imagine the strength it was taking to hold onto the cable. Jade did not hesitate and activated the winch at half speed reverse.

"I need you to confirm when you are in the cargo hold," Jade explained eyeballing the oncoming space fighters. She expected to have visual at any moment. "I can't get up to come to help you."

There was a pause. "Not that I need help, but why is that exactly?" Sal asked, her voice suspicious. Jade contemplated not telling her as the woman needed to focus on staying attached to the cable. In the end, she did not need to decide. The A0406 craft was now in view. Again, the commlink crackled. "Tell me these are long lost buddies of yours, Jade," Sal said.

Jade wished she could.

CHAPTER 11
SAL

By the time Sal reached the trapdoor in the hull of the starship, her arms were screaming. Even though she hooked the cable to her utility belt, the impact of grabbing it initially was almost enough to dislocate her shoulders. *And I still wouldn't have let go*, she thought. Falling off the roof was not on her agenda. Sal sure as hell was not going to allow whoever set her up to get away with it. As she pulled herself aboard and stood up in the cargo hold, the sound of blaring alarms from the cockpit greeted her. *What the hell is this crap with the fighters all about? Could this mission get any more screwed up?*

After disconnecting herself from the cable and rotating her arms in their sockets as she walked, Sal moved to the front of the starship only to see Jade working the console to activate the autopilot evasion maneuvers. "So, let me get this straight," Sal said. "We are being attacked." Jade jumped in her seat, obviously not having heard Sal come into the cockpit behind her.

Jade glanced over her shoulder. "You don't need to be up here," she snapped.

Sal narrowed her eyes. "That's not answering my question," she said. "Are we being attacked?"

"Not exactly," Jade answered without looking at Sal. "Or at least I don't think so."

Sal sighed. She could tell the woman was only being stubborn and was not ready to admit yet they were being double-crossed. Sal leaned forward to see over Jade's shoulder and examined the radar. After a pause, she snorted a laugh. *Ridiculous,* she thought and a little perturbed the bad guys were giving her such little credit. *They are certainly obvious about their approach.* Leaning even closer to Jade, she smiled when the woman stiffened. If things were not going to shit so fast, Sal would have enjoyed playing with her more, but for now, she pointed at the two blips flashing on the screen.

"So, these guys are what? Our escort?" Sal asked, her voice dripping with sarcasm.

"And what if they are?" Jade answered. "But until they identify themselves, I thought we should at least take an evasion maneuver."

Sal nodded giving Jade a little credit for not leaving them as sitting ducks. "What happens when you commlink to them?" Sal asked as she slipped into the seat beside Jade and reached for the second set of steering apparatus.

"They don't answer," Jade said without looking over. Sal saw the woman's jaw tighten. *Just trying to deny to herself that we are screwed,* Sal thought. *But we don't have time for that right now.* Sal activated her steering controls and turned off the automatic evasion maneuvers. She also reached over and canceled all of the alarms. The sudden quiet in the cabin was blessed.

"What the hell do you think you're doing?" Jade snapped, this time turning to glare at Sal. Sal gave her a cocky smile.

"Saving our butts," Sal answered while she pulled up an orbital positioning system outlining the solar system surrounding their immediate area.

"If you think you're piloting, you're mistaken. That is not part of this mission," Jade said and started to reach over and turn off Sal's controls. Sal grabbed her by the wrist and held it in place. Their eyes locked.

"Do you mean the mission where the president of the 8th Galaxy was already dead, and I had to jump out the window?" Sal asked quietly. "You know, the one where I was shot at, not to mention about knocked off the building? Or wait, maybe the same one where some bogies are now running up our ass?" Jade only glared at her and, after a pause, Sal chuckled. She loved being right, especially in the face of someone who thought they were superior.

"Fine," Jade snapped as she yanked her arm back breaking Sal's loose grip. "But I think you're overreacting. This is only a misunderstanding."

"Forgive me for not being so naive, Jade. Now if you don't mind letting me do my thing," Sal said as she checked her visual on the fighters who would be on them within the next few seconds if she did not get a move on. She had never flown a P-527 but found it adequate. Not as fast as a Space Ranger fighter unfortunately and nothing compared to the space pirate ships they souped up after capturing them. Still, she knew she could make it work. "Let's see what this baby can do," she whispered under her breath pushing the thrusters and throwing the starship into a dive back toward the surface of the planet.

"Seriously," Jade said gripping the armrests of her seat. "Where do you think you're going?"

"I need to find some cover," Sal replied. "If I try to blast past them to get into outer space, they will run us down, and that'll be the end of that." As Sal plunged the spaceship down at the planet and back in the direction of the compound, she noticed the fighters responding immediately. What they undoubtedly thought was a sitting duck mission was suddenly turning against them. Out of the corner of her eye, Sal watched them react as blips on her radar, knowing the two faster ships would be in a position to lock on them quickly. Even Sal admitted this presented something of a problem, considering the desert planet provided little to hide behind. *Then back to the compound it is,* she thought and spun them in a spiral to head directly toward the walls of the enclosure. She felt Jade's hand on her arm. "Sal, seriously, what are you thinking?" she asked, and Sal chuckled.

"I think it's time to make a little run down the middle of Main Street," she said as she raced over the chain-link fence around the compound and snapped a turn between the first two buildings. The timing was perfect as a laser cannon blast from one of the fighters took out a chunk of the building to her left. She heard Jade suck in her breath, apparently realizing if Sal had not made the turn when she did, they would be toast.

"Jesus," Jade whispered. "What is happening?"

"Believe me now?" Sal said as she navigated back and forth between more buildings, rotating the ship from left to right on its axis, shaking them both from side to side in their seats. Jade shook her head, but Sal knew it was now more from disbelief than doubt. At that moment, another laser blast blew by, this time to the right and as debris from the taller building fell against the side of their ship, Sal spun them hard to avoid the entire collapsing wall of concrete. Racing down the last strip of the road, with only a few buildings left before they were back out in the open desert, Sal knew the fighters were close. She needed to think of something, and she had to think of it now or else the game was up. There would be no cover in the desert beyond the fence. Glancing left and right, she realized there was still one option. "Buckle in tight," Sal said. The woman's eyes widened, but she pulled on the straps to make sure she was well seated.

"What are you going to do?" she asked, but Sal did not bother to answer. There was no time. Slamming the thrusters all the way forward to get them every ounce of speed the ship might still have, she rocketed them along, and as she cleared the last corner of the buildings, ripped the ship hard to the left. Twisting the craft vertical, the centrifugal force of holding the turn threw both of them back against their seats. The ship screamed around the building, keeping a circle so close they nicked the final corner of the structure as Sal spun around it in a perfect radial turn. As they shot through the alley back onto the main drag, Sal saw what she wanted and grinned. Straight in front of her were the two fighters who were on their tail until a moment before. The pilots had no time to react to her turn, and now she was right up their tailpipes.

"Hello, Rangers," Sal said as she switched on the laser cannon to full power and blasted the first starfighter into oblivion. As they shot through the shrapnel of the now destroyed craft, Sal saw the fighter in the front take an evasive spin, trying to make its way back up off of the deck. "Oh, no you don't," Sal growled. She pushed the P-527 ship with all the strength she had left in the thrusters. Knowing her only chance was to try taking a diagonal which would let her intercept the smaller craft, she lifted the nose of her ship. She knew the smaller fighter had more power, but by going almost straight up, she thought she could catch him as he crossed her line of fire. It would give her only one shot, and she smiled. *Those are precisely the kind of odds I like the most*, she thought and turned to smile at Jade. Seeing her look, Jade furrowed her brow.

"What?" she asked.

Sal raised an eyebrow. "I'll bet you a dinner on Prospo I get him with one shot," Sal said.

"You can't be serious?" Jade responded with a shake of her head. "Maybe you should—"

"I'm dead serious," Sal answered. "Unless you'd like to bet something else?" They insinuation was thick in her voice, and she saw Jade blush the moment before Sal pulled the trigger to fire the laser cannon. It indeed was a beautiful shot, and Sal turned back to watch the blast strike home. As she watched the fireball, she felt a sliver of regret that some poor pair of Space Rangers gave their life for something so dirty as a double-cross. Then, she shook her head knowing that kind of thinking would get her nowhere. *It was them or us*, she thought, and in the end, Salishan Bransen did not give a rat's ass about anyone. Ever.

CHAPTER 12
JADE

Nothing made sense. Jade held her breath as she watched the second starfighter explode and knew something was incredibly wrong. Two ships destroyed, two pilots unnecessarily dead, but Sal had no choice, and Jade knew it. *They were going to kill us*, she thought with a shake of her head trying to clear the confusion. She felt Sal steer their spaceship into a smoother ascent, yet when she looked, they were headed away from any trajectory to rendezvous with their space carrier. "Where are you going?" she asked.

Sal glanced over at her. "Open space. I think our hull may have taken damage when part of the second building hit us. I don't know how long this thing is going to hold together, so I'm making the most of what we have to leave right now. Unless you want to get stuck on this planet."

Jade frowned. "No, of course not," she said. "But we need to go back to our prearranged destination."

"Like hell I am," Sal answered without even bothering to glance Jade's way. "Were you not paying attention? They tried to blow us out of the sky."

Jade shook her head. "No, there has to be some mix-up," she replied. "Obviously, two parties were working on the same objective, and we need to get it straightened out."

Sal barked out a laugh. "I think you misunderstand the real objective in this case," she said. "I was set up. Or more accurately, we were set up, and you need to find a way to get your head around it." Jade watched Sal make some adjustments to settings on the console. "Now if you don't mind, I'm trying to get us far enough away to buy time until we figure out what to do next."

Jade heard enough. She was in charge of this mission. *And I'll be damned if I am going to let some rogue agent tell me what is going to happen next,* she thought. "Ranger Salishan Bransen, I am ordering you to turn this ship around and go back to the rendezvous point. Is that clear?"

Sal remained silent for a moment staring out the windshield as she kept the ship racing along toward outer space. The minute stretched so long Jade thought she might not even answer, and she was about to repeat herself when Sal slowly looked at her.

"I am refusing your order," she said. "Out of your best interest as well as mine. You do realize they intended to shoot down the ship with both of us on board?"

Jade sucked in a breath and held it, not ready to believe what Sal told her. She was a well-respected senior agent and an experienced Space Ranger. She was decorated for her achievements and could not believe she would be so easily sacrificed. *I am not expendable. Or at least I don't think so*, she thought feeling a bit of unease creep into her chest. *What if they really were trying to kill both of us?* "No," she finally stated. "You're wrong. I am ordering you one more time to turn the ship around."

She saw Sal clench her jaw, turning to look back out the windshield, but waited for her to obey. After all, Jade was the superior officer. This was her mission. Sal was her agent. Again, the moment drug on, but finally Sal shrugged as if she did not have a care in the world. "You'll have to shoot me if you want to turn this ship around," she murmured. Jade could hardly believe her ears. *This is outrageous*, she thought, and yet in her mind and even in her heart, she knew without a doubt Sal was entirely sincere.

Not sure what to do next, Jade leaned back in her seat and contemplated her next move. As she did so the commlink crackled to life. *Finally*, she thought. *Someone is sending us a transmission which will sort out this mess.* Unfortunately, the words coming over the transmission were not from the space carrier. It was an all-points bulletin. As she listened, her heart grew cold.

"This is an 8th Galaxy-wide emergency bulletin ..." the mechanical voice reported. "In association with the reported assassination of President Franmiller, two suspects are now wanted for immediate questioning ..."

Leaning forward now, waiting with bated breath for the next sentence, Jade already knew what she was about to hear. "Space Ranger Captain Salishan Bransen and Space Ranger Senior Agent Jade Hamilton meeting the description of ..." A ringing started in Jade's ears as she tried to absorb the news. *They are labeling us as assassins!* she thought. *Of the president!* She knew every resource in the law enforcement field, as well as bounty hunters no doubt, would be searching for them. *With plans to shoot to kill.*

Jade braced herself for Sal's "I told you so" but when it did not come, she looked and saw Sal was staring out the windshield. Her face was unreadable, and Jade could only guess what she was thinking. *The Space Ranger Corps have turned their back on her a second time*, she thought. *Abandoned all over again after doing something they assigned her to do.* Even filled with fear at their current situation, Jade felt a tug of sympathy for the woman. *But doesn't Sal deserve this in a way? For all the evil she did?* Jade was not sure anymore, and that was the last thing she wanted to feel conflicted about right now. There could be no sympathy in her heart for Sal. Jade would not let it. Still, she knew she had to say something. "I'm sorry," Jade finally said.

For a moment, Sal did not reply and then she chuckled. "I'm not," she said. "This is a lot more fun. Now if you don't mind being a good copilot, can you pull up the orbital positioning system and figure out the closest wormhole we can hyperspace through?"

Jade blinked, not sure what to make of the request. Sensing Jade's hesitation, Sal raised an eyebrow. "Problem?" she asked. Slowly understanding dawned on Jade, and she shook her head.

"You want to run to an unexplored corner of the galaxy before they capture us," Jade responded, quickly tapping the screen to pull up the digital display of all sectors. Swiping her hand from left to right to scroll across different portions of the universe, she paused when she came to a blurry area. It was an uninhabited planet cluster. *Or at least unexplored*, she thought, knowing that simply because the 8th Galaxy alliance had yet to settle those planets did not mean no life existed there.

"Quickly," Sal said. "We're running out of time and I need to get us into another orbit before a new batch of fighters is up our ass."

Without a lot of time to analyze where they might want to land, Jade quickly picked a medium-sized planet of blue-green swirls. She recognized white ribbons which indicated the atmosphere and a high probability of sustaining humanoid lifeforms. Assuming her memory of what she learned at the academy was accurate, she pointed to it. "Let's go here," she said. "It's 173482–B11." Sal only glanced at it before she nodded.

"Tap in our trajectory and let's go. We're going to need to pick up speed to make a jump to hyperspace," she said.

"I thought you said the hull took damage. Do you think that is a good idea?" Jade asked, filled with uncertainty as the tremor in the ship continue to increase the faster their speed.

"There's only one way to find out," Sal said. "Type it in."

Jade complied. "Ready," she said in almost a whisper, feeling her heart race at the idea anything could happen next. She watched Sal reach for the throttle to launch them, but then her hand hesitated, and Jade thought for a moment the woman was uncertain of their chances. Then, she saw Sal shake her head as if undecided about something else entirely. Before Jade could ask, she watched the woman reached over and change the commlink to a different channel. It was far to one end of the frequency spectrum and not something Jade was familiar with. *A private, somehow obscured channel?* Jade wondered, and then Sal began to speak.

"This transmission is top secret clearance only," Sal said. "Encrypted message to Catwoman. Start. 173482–B11. Stop."

With that, Sal clicked off and returned her hand to the throttle to launch them into hyperspace.

"What was that for?" Jade asked, not sure she understood the point of giving someone a random number, even if it was a planet identifier. *Is there someone out there that Sal thinks she can trust after all?* she wondered in time to see Sal push her hand forward to launch them into hyperspace and toward the coordinates of the wormhole and beyond.

"Just hang on," Sal said by way of answer and Jade gripped the armrests as the ship picked up speed. It was quite possible they were both about to die, and Jade had one random thought. If this was the end, she wished Sal kissed her first. Then, they blasted into parts unknown.

CHAPTER 13
NAT

The elite 33-70 fighter spaceship handled beautifully as Captain Natalie (Nat) Reynolds flew through the inky blackness of space. Never was there a newer, more expensive craft at her disposal and as she goosed the thrusters, she took pleasure in the way she was pressed back in her seat. *I could get used to this*, she thought with a grin and took the machine in a broad looping arc. As she crested the top, her commlink light flashed on the dashboard a moment before her friend Dee, a Space Ranger dispatcher, gave her call sign. "Base to Cat-woman," the woman's voice said. Nat finished her swing and leveled out as she pressed the screen at her fingertips.

"Go ahead, Base," she answered and waited for her next assignment. As a Space Ranger in the 8th Galaxy, there was always something, and everything was quiet all morning. *What will it be?* she wondered. *A stranded ship? A distress call from people in trouble?* Her grin broadened. *Or something more exciting like an intruder in the controlled airspace of a nearby planet?* In the end, the mission did not matter. She loved her job and the excitement every moment brought with it.

Realizing Base was not answering, Nat keyed the link again. "Base? Go ahead with the transmission," she said and was relieved when the woman's voice sounded again. Only this time, her message was confusing.

"Wake up, sweetheart," the dispatcher said. "Time to go save the world." Nat frowned. She liked the save the world part. *But aren't I already awake?* she wondered. Suddenly, a warm hand was touching her cheek, and the sensation was unexpected, but not unpleasant. "Come on, baby," the woman said, and this time Nat felt her reality shift. As the wisps of her dream melted away, Nat blinked open her eyes to look into a beautiful, young woman's face. She was standing beside the bed leaning over her. Nat's heart swelled at the sight. She was the woman she loved.

"Good morning, Catherine," Nat said and playfully grabbed her by the waist to pull her onto the bed. Catherine giggled but put her hands on Nat's wrists as she struggled to keep her feet.

"Didn't you get enough of me last night?" she asked with a blush.

"Never," Nat growled and reached again. She would like nothing more than to take Catherine again. Somehow, she always seemed to want her. Catherine laughed and slapped her hands away, although the desire in her eyes let Nat know she could have her right now if she insisted. The heat between them never cooled.

"I promise later," she said licking her lips. "But there are eager young cadets waiting for you to come and fill their minds with your Space Ranger wisdom."

Ah yes, Nat thought, feeling fully awake and grounded in reality. She was a trainer at the planet's Space Ranger Academy. That day she would be working with a team of trainers to run two units of recruits through an elaborate obstacle course. This was the third time she participated in the six months she was with the academy, and Nat found it a highlight. The rest of the training, however, was mundane in her opinion. Nat would never admit it to Catherine, but being a trainer was boring, especially compared to what she wished to be doing. Her old career called to her like a siren song, yet the only way she could see keeping the woman she loved happy was to continue on her present course. Losing Catherine was not an option. If anything, Nat wanted to make their relationship more permanent. Yet, anytime she alluded to the idea of marriage, Catherine quickly changed the subject. Nat could only hope over time she would warm up to the idea. At the moment though, she needed to get in the shower.

Nat sat and swung her long, muscular legs over the side of the bed. They were bare, and a thick, pink scar marked a repaired injury on her knee. Shrapnel from an explosion she created was once embedded there. The pain was well worth it though. She was able to help bring down the cloaking mechanism of a space pirate hideout as well as make it possible for her and Catherine to escape. That morning the bionic knee replacement felt stiff. *Is this damn thing acting up again?* she thought having never been pleased with the device. Sometimes she wondered if the replacement was simply a lemon and should be swapped out. The current problem was not something she wanted to address just then though, as another six months of rehab was out of the question in her mind. *It's not like I do much on it anyway sitting behind a damn desk.* Nat frowned and knew the bad knee was only another reminder of her limitations. Space Rangers pilots were required to be in top physical condition, and Nat knew she would not be able to pass an examination. Or at least not yet.

"Want me to bring your coffee into the bathroom while you shower?" Catherine asked as she turned toward their apartment's small kitchen. She did not notice Nat's frustrated expression.

Standing up, Nat did her best to hide a limp as she made her way to the bathroom to start her day. "That would be perfect," she answered forcing a cheerful tone into her voice. "You're sure you don't want to join me?" Pausing at the door, Catherine tossed a smile back her way, and Nat grinned. Seeing her happy was all Nat needed. The last thing she wanted was to worry Catherine. The situation was not her fault, but she knew sometimes the young woman thought so. Nat was pretty sure it was one of the reasons she refused to talk about marriage.

"Behave yourself, Captain," Catherine replied, but her voice had a huskier tone than before, and Nat knew what her lover was thinking. The first time they made love was in a shower, and it continued to be one of their favorite places. With a chuckle, Nat continued toward the bathroom.

"Yes, dear," she said and then heard Catherine giggling as she left the bedroom.

The shower was hot and helped her relax. The coffee Catherine brought in for her was strong and bold, exactly the way she liked it. She was putting on her trainer's uniform when Catherine came in. "Nat," she said sounding a touch concerned. "Dee is on the commlink for you." Nat could understand why

Catherine might be worried. Their friend would not contact her so early in the morning unless something were amiss. Following Catherine into the living room, Nat saw Dee's face on the large monitor on the wall.

"Good morning, Dee," Nat said. "What's going on?"

Nat watched Dee glance in Catherine's direction and then she cleared her throat. "Maybe we can take this on the handset?" she suggested. Nat felt Catherine come up beside her and was conflicted. She trusted the woman completely, but if the information was top secret fleet information ... *But why in the world would Dee, a senior Space Ranger dispatcher as well as a friend, be calling me at 0700 for something like that?* she wondered. *I'm just a trainer.* Nat made a split decision to let Catherine listen in.

"You can speak freely," she advised. "I'll vouch for Catherine."

She saw Dee shrug on the screen. "Okay," she said. "But don't blame me if you wish you hadn't." Nat frowned. *What the hell is this about?* she thought and was starting to become truly worried. Then, a thought struck her. There was one topic she actually might want to keep Catherine from hearing. Not because she did not trust her, but instead because it could upset her.

"Wait," Nat interrupted. "Is this about an ex-Space Ranger?" At the question, Nat felt Catherine stiffen. There was no doubt she knew the person Nat was referring to and out of protective instinct, Nat put her arm around the petite woman's shoulders.

"Has something happened to Sal?" Catherine asked softly. "Is she ..." Her voice trailed off, but Nat knew what the question would have been. With someone as crazy and dangerous as Salishan Bransen, she could not ignore the likelihood Sal was dead. Both the Space Rangers, and probably assassins hired by the space pirates, were looking high and low for her.

"She's not dead if that's what you're thinking," Dee answered, and Nat heard Catherine let out a breath. "But apparently, she's in deep shit. There's an APB out on her."

Nat raised her eyebrows. "An all-points bulletin out on Sal?" she asked.

She watched Dee nod. "Yes," she said. "They are saying Sal assassinated the president of the 8th Galaxy, Nat."

Nat raised her eyebrows in surprise. She knew the woman was dangerous, but this news was incredible. "No," Catherine murmured from beside her. "She would never do that." Thinking it over, Nat wondered if maybe she was right. *What would Sal gain from doing such a thing?* she thought knowing the woman never did anything unless she benefited.

She felt Catherine take her hand and squeeze making Nat look down into her face. A myriad of emotions played over the woman's beautiful features. "You know it's not true, Nat," she said. "You of all people must know it."

Nat paused to consider Catherine's words. Ever since they all escaped from the space pirate's hideout months ago, Catherine insisted Sal and Nat were kindred spirits. *Two sides to the same coin. One dark, one light, but made from the same metal,* Nat remembered. Although Nat always laughed and told Catherine she was romanticizing things, even she could admit there was an undeniable, albeit strange, connection between them. *Yes, she is right.* She did know Sal would not assassinate anyone unless there was a very good reason. She looked at Dee on the monitor.

"Where is she?" Nat asked although it could be on the next planet over and she still would have no way to get there unless it was by public transport. As a trainer, she did not have her own ship anymore. It was a fact which grated on her often, but like everything else about her current situation, she swallowed the disappointment and did not let on.

"That is a good question," Dee said. "The entire fleet is looking for her, but it appears she hit a wormhole and is long gone."

CHAPTER 14
CATHERINE

When she heard Dee say Sal's name, Catherine's heart nearly stopped. The woman was missing for months and even though there was no reason to expect Sal would ever contact her, a part of Catherine always hoped to hear somehow that she was all right. Sal was important to her, and Catherine knew she owed the ex-Ranger her life. Although Nat was the only woman she would ever love, Sal held a special place in Catherine's heart, too. *And now she is in trouble,* she thought. *But at least she is alive.* Catherine knew Sal was quite possibly, aside from Nat, the most resourceful person in the galaxy. Still, she was a fugitive from the Space Rangers and no doubt a target for lingering space pirates. But, when she heard Dee explaining Sal was wanted for assassinating the president, she almost could not breathe. It was simply not possible. *We have to do something to help her.*

As she pondered what to do next, she heard Nat signing off with Dee. "Keep me posted if you hear anything else, okay?" Nat asked, and Catherine watched Dee nod on the monitor.

"You got it, but I'm not expecting anything. Sal is a slippery one. Still, a lot of folks think Sal disgraced the Space Rangers with how she acted while undercover with the pirates," she said. "And now this? You and I both know people will be shooting to kill."

Catherine's eyes widened. This was the last thing she wanted to hear. "No," Catherine blurted. "Sal did what she had to in order to survive. And you both know she would never do this." Nat kissed the top of her head to console her, but Catherine did not want to be comforted. She pulled back and looked up at Nat wanting them to help Sal. "Certainly, there is something we can do," Catherine insisted. Neither woman seemed to know what to say.

Finally, Nat nodded. "I'll see what I can find out from some of my old contacts within the Rangers," she said. "No promises."

Catherine nodded and looked at Dee. "Well?" Catherine said.

Dee and Catherine never quite saw eye-to-eye as both women were especially protective of Nat. Dee made no effort to hide the fact she was waiting to see if Catherine would stick or if Nat was going to have her heart broken again. Finally, the woman shrugged. "So will I, but as Nat said. No promises," she replied. "I need to sign off. Take care of yourselves."

"Same to you," Nat answered, and then the screen went blank. For a moment, they both stood there and looked at the monitor, each digesting the information.

Catherine hated to think of what Sal might be facing right now. "I know you won't promise, but please try and help her," she murmured. "For me."

"Sal made her bed, and now she has to sleep in it," Nat explained. "I agree, we owe her a debt, but other than ask around, I can't do much for her. I'm nothing but a trainer now."

Catherine felt her heart sink. She was not sure what she wanted to happen next, but somehow, she knew Sal needed to be saved. With a sigh, she put her arms around Nat's waist and leaned into her. "I know," she agreed. "It all seems so unfair to her." They were quiet for a moment and then Nat ran a hand over Catherine's hair.

"I have to go," she said, and Catherine nodded against her chest before giving her one last squeeze.

"I know," she said as she let go. "Be safe, okay?" Nat smiled and kissed her. The peck was supposed to be tender, yet with the news about Sal and the reality anything could happen, Catherine took it deeper in an instant. Suddenly, she wanted nothing more than to rip Nat's uniform off. They finally broke away with a gasp. Nat's eyes were hungry, and Catherine knew her feelings were the same, yet as was always the case with Nat, duty came first.

"Hold that thought," she said.

Catherine smiled. "I most definitely will."

AFTER NAT LEFT, CATHERINE felt frustration settle in. Making herself a cup of coffee, she went to the couch and ran through everything she knew. For starters, she did not believe for a second what people were saying about Sal was true. The woman did things in the past, Catherine was not naïve enough to pretend were not horrible, but they were all part of her need to survive while undercover. Those actions did not equate to her suddenly deciding to kill the president of the 8th Galaxy. *If she was there, someone has to be setting her up*, Catherine thought as she considered all the facts. *But who? And why? Revenge?*

Taking a sip, she narrowed her eyes and considered Sal's enemies. She knew the Space Rangers hated Sal because of her past actions. Nat said once that some Rangers felt embarrassed by what Sal did to tarnish their image. Yet, the idea they were involved did not make sense. If the Rangers knew where Sal was, in proximity to where the president was assassinated, why didn't they capture Sal outright? *What is the point of telling the world she is an assassin?* she wondered. She already had a price on her head, and although this new situation made Sal's life worse, Catherine could not follow the logic.

Which left space pirates. *Could the space pirates somehow have devised a plan to make it look like Salishan Bransen assassinated the president?* she wondered. Most of the pirate's leadership were captured when the Space Rangers overran the hideaway after Nat and Sal brought down their cloaking device. The Space Rangers responded in force to the emergency call, and she knew from things Nat said later, the mission significantly diminished the strength of the space pirates and their control over the galaxy. She found it hard to believe they were in a position to pull off something like this.

So, if it isn't the Space Rangers and it isn't the space pirates, who could it be? she wondered setting the coffee on the table. No answer came to her, but she knew why was not what she needed to focus on right now. More important was trying to figure out where Sal was hiding. Catherine was savvy enough to know with Sal being on the run, with the whole galaxy looking for her, she would need to go somewhere outside the typically populated planet boundaries. *That leaves a lot of places though*, she thought. It seemed like it would be impossible to figure out where the woman was hiding, and although that was a good thing in the sense neither Rangers nor pirates could get to her, it also meant Catherine or even Nat could not help.

And I very much want to help, she thought. *And I know Nat will too.* Although the woman made it sound like she did not care what happened to Sal, even acting like she might believe the woman committed the crime, Catherine did not believe it. There was a bond between them, and she felt in her heart Nat would never turn her back on the ex-Ranger. *We have to find her!*

Deciding to get dressed to go out and do some of her own research, she heard the ping of Nat's commlink device. Following the sound, Catherine found it on the counter beside the bathroom sink. In her rush to get to the academy after being delayed by Dee's call, Nat forgot it. Picking the device up, Catherine looked at the screen and saw a blinking red alert. This was new. She never saw such a thing on any commlink. Curious, she tapped on the icon, but all she could see was who the message was addressed to and no other details. The rest appeared encrypted. Those details did not matter to Catherine as the word at the top of the screen made her heart stop for a moment. The message was addressed to Catwoman and Catherine had no doubt in her mind who sent it. It would be Sal. *I have to get this to Nat right now*, Catherine thought moving to the closet and grabbing clothes. Sal reached out to Nat after all, and Catherine was going to make sure the message was delivered.

CHAPTER 15
SAL

Going hyperdrive through a wormhole was never a lot of fun. It hurtled a person along at an incomprehensible speed, only to spit the ship out at the end with God only knew what in its path. In this case, for Sal, it was a bright green and blue planet rushing up at her so fast, she barely had time to level the shuddering starship out as it breached the atmosphere. She heard Jade blow out a breath of relief in the seat beside her. *I don't blame her*, Sal thought. *We could just as easily shoot through there only to end up playing chicken with an asteroid.*

The moment she thought they might make it to the surface of the planet for a soft landing, the panel of the starship lit up like a Christmas parade. Alarms blared, and a mechanical voice, Sal hated whenever she heard it, began to announce a dooms-day scenario. "Impact in five minutes at this trajectory. Advise to pull up," the voice claimed. *As if I couldn't figure that out myself*, Sal thought as she struggled with the sluggish controls. "Jade," Sal said. "I need you to run an atmospheric analysis right now."

Jade did not even take the time to answer as she immediately pulled up the display which allowed her to filter the outside air through a computer bank to determine oxygen levels and other critical particulars of the planet. If the air was not something they could breathe, they would need to get in their spacesuits immediately. Sal was against the idea of suiting up as it would take time and right now, as the God damned voice was reminding her, they had four minutes before impact.

Jade's hands flew across the console. Sal watched her out of the corner of her eye, impressed about how cool and calm the woman was considering their circumstances. In a little over a hundred and eighty seconds, the ship was on the ground one way or the other. *Not bad*, Sal thought. *Not bad at all.*

As the planet's canopy of green, broad-leafed trees raced toward them, Sal used all her strength to pull back to level out the hurtling mass of their spaceship, which threatened to come apart at the seams. "Atmospheric levels are within range to support human life," Jade reported with relief evident in her voice. "It does not advise space suits."

"Perfect," Sal answered as she felt the ship slowly start to pull up enough to get them a hint of a glide.

The mechanical voice was unimpressed. "Impact in three minutes. Advise pull up," the voice screeched at them at the same time the first tops of the trees began to scrape the bottom of the starship.

"Hang on," Sal said, and out of the corner of her eye, she watched as Jade grabbed the armrests of her seat. The woman leaned as far back into the cushions as she could as if trying to will the racing ship higher over the trees.

No such luck, Sal thought as they started to sink lower. Branches begin to slap them, and she felt the first tearing of the hull. *Probably one of the wings pulling loose.* Sal knew even though the obnoxious voice gave them two minutes to impact they would be lucky to go that long.

"Oh shit," she heard Jade whisper and Sal had to agree. Things did not look good.

Just then, the ship cleared the last of the jungle and came out over a large crystal blue lake. It was such a welcome surprise, Sal laughed. *Oh, this I can deal with*, she thought, as the ship continued to sink lower. Wrestling with the failing starship, she aimed for the lake with the plan to skim the water surface as much as possible. Anything but a headfirst plunge. "Please tell me you did your check down protocol before takeoff earlier and can confirm this thing has a life raft," Sal said. Out of the corner of her eye, she saw Jade nod. The woman's face was pale, and she looked almost queasy. "But let me guess, you're not much of a swimmer?"

Jade swallowed hard and shook her head. "No, I am not," Jade answered.

"Well, then don't get too far away from me," Sal advised, as the starship touched down and a spray of white water shot over the windshield. Sal was thrown against the seat restraints as the ship came to a rapid halt from the force of the water. Immediately, the computer voice screeched, filling the cabin. "Alert! Impact," it said.

No shit, Sherlock, Sal thought as she felt her shoulders already starting to ache from where the seatbelts held her. There was going to be a hell of a bruise. Looking over, she checked to see if Jade was okay. The woman was rubbing her chest where the belts crisscrossed, but otherwise seemed fine. "Well, that was a hell of a landing," Sal laughed as she started to unfasten her seatbelts.

"Do you always have to make a joke about everything?" Jade asked as she followed suit.

"Who said I was joking?" Sal answered as she climbed out of the seat and started toward the cargo area. Water was already seeping in through the places where the craft took damage as it plunged through the trees. *It's not going to stay afloat for long*, she thought and began reaching for supplies from the different cabinets. Slinging a laser rifle over her shoulder, she spotted the container marked "raft" and threw it toward the door in the side of the hull.

Jade splashed toward her through the rising water. "Want to figure out how to work that thing?" Sal asked with a glance at the raft. Jade looked at her blankly, and Sal knew the woman was not far from going into shock. It was the last thing she needed. Reaching out, she grabbed Jade by the shoulder and gave her a little shake. "Hello? Untas to Jade?" Sal said into her face. The woman blinked, and Sal leaned in closer until they were nose-to-nose. "Listen, beautiful. I think we have about one minute before this thing is so far in the water, we won't get any doors open. Time to wake up." Sal was not sure which part of what she said registered, but suddenly Jade's eyes widened.

"Okay," Jade murmured.

Sal winked. "Good, now, figure out the raft," she said pointing at the now floating bag. Jade nodded as she stepped over to begin reading the display on the side of the raft's packaging.

Pushing a button, the thing started to speak to her. "Do not inflate until outside of the craft," an earnest voice clipped. "I repeat, do not deploy until outside the craft." Seemed like good advice to Sal. She reached into more cabinets and found a duffel bag full of first-aid and other survival supplies. Considering she did not have any way of knowing how long they would be on the planet, she knew every single thing she could grab now would come in handy later.

"I can't get the door open," Jade said from behind her and Sal glanced over as she slung the duffel bag's strap over her shoulder already holding the rifle. In a glance, she knew the electrical circuits in the ship failed and now the control panel to open the door was dead. *Of course*, Sal thought. *This cluster fuck only seems to get better.*

"Stand back," Sal instructed.

"What are you going to do?" Jade started, but before she could finish the sentence, Sal yanked her plasma gun from the holster and fired two shots into the side of the hull to the left of the door. A large opening appeared and water immediately started to rush in. "Why did you do that?" Jade asked. "Why not blast the door?"

"Because they reinforce it against attack," Sal said as she pushed through the knee-deep water toward the opening. "Geniuses who made these things didn't seem to realize someone might think to shoot to the side of the door." She stopped beside the gap in the hull. "Bring the raft over."

As Jade pulled it closer, struggling in the water almost to her waist, Sal reached to help her. "Do not deploy inside," the instructions chimed again, and Sal was sick and tired of mechanical voices telling her what to do. She pressed the activate button while swinging the clunky parcel through the hole. It immediately started to inflate, and Sal knew it would be floating away from them in seconds.

"Okay, time to go," she said.

Jade froze. "I don't think I can do it," she whispered.

"I think you can," Sal said with no patience. In about two more minutes, the cargo hold would fill to the ceiling. "Get on my back."

"On your back?" Jade asked, still standing in one spot.

"Yes, get on my back. Right now," Sal said, but Jade still looked like a deer in headlights. *Oh, for God's sake,* Sal thought and took one step to Jade before grabbing her up like a sack of potatoes and tossing her over her shoulder. Jade let out a little chirp of surprise but otherwise did not resist.

"Oof," Sal said, now carrying the rifle, a full duffel bag, and a woman. *I'm more out of shape than I thought,* she realized as she moved to the edge of the opening, saw the raft floating away, and lunged out of the starship.

CHAPTER 16
JADE

As a decorated officer in the Space Ranger Corps, Jade faced many things which would scare the average person to the point they could not go any further, but she always faced them down—except for one thing. Water. Falling into the water petrified Jade. When the starship headed toward the lake, her heart nearly stopped. If she had been able to catch her breath, she would have explained to Sal she would rather crash in the trees than risk submerging. Somehow, Sal was able to keep them from diving under the surface and for that alone Jade would be eternally grateful.

Yet, when water rushed in, and Sal blasted a hole in the side of the ship, not to mention throwing their one and only raft outside, Jade's panic rushed back. Add in the woman was telling her to jump on her back, and Jade froze. Sal was leaving the ship and wanted to take Jade into the water. She was not sure she could do it, but in the end, Jade did not get to decide. Sal lifted her, slung her unceremoniously over her shoulder, and threw them both out of the opening.

They landed in a heap on the edge of the already inflated raft, and when Sal wavered on the spongy rubber surface, Jade clenched her teeth to keep from screaming. Their position was precariously perched and at any second Sal could fall backward into the water. With her extra weight, Jade knew she was making it harder for Sal to keep her balance, but in her position she was helpless. The water was inches from her face, and her ass was up in the air. Then, with a grunt, she felt Sal rock them forward, and Jade was suddenly thrown onto the bottom of the raft. Unable to stop her momentum, Sal landed on top of her. Through her fear, or perhaps because of it, Jade's core bloomed with unexpected heat as she thought about how close her body pressed to the other woman's. Amid all the craziness swirling around her, a primal need to touch Sal or even more to be touched by Sal came over her.

As an ache started between her legs, breath hitching at the images flowing through her mind, she felt Sal lift her head to look down at Jade. Their eyes met, and Jade could tell Sal knew what she was thinking. Jade bit her lip not sure what might happen next. *Are we going to do this?* she wondered. *Right here on this raft? What am I thinking?* Then, there was a bump. From underneath the raft. "What was that?" she asked, her desire suddenly extinguished by fear.

"Good question," Sal answered and pushed herself up to look around. Jade followed suit, only to look over the edge and see a dark shape near the raft. *Please let that be rocks*, she thought.

"Do you see that?" Jade asked, pointing at the object.

"It's rocks," Sal said. "But let's get to the beach." Tearing her eyes away from the sight, Jade looked around and saw a sandy spot less than a hundred meters away.

"Can we go there?" she asked, noticing Sal was already moving to the raft's propulsion controls.

"Yep," Sal answered activating the starter for the turbo propeller that would push them along the water. Jade moved to the bow, returning her eyes to the dark shape. She took solace in the fact it did not appear to have moved since she noticed it. *Definitely rocks*, she thought ready to be off the water soon. Jade started to relax when suddenly the dark shape did precisely what she had prayed it would not. It shifted.

"Sal," Jade said as fear tightened her throat. "It moved."

"Yep, saw that," Sal said. It was so nonchalant, Jade glanced up at her. Even at that moment, while they rode across the lake on an unexplored planet with God knew what under the surface, Sal was not fazed. *Does anything ever get to this woman?* she thought praying they would survive long enough for her to find out.

As Jade gripped the side of the raft and felt it pick up speed bumping along the top of the water, she kept her eyes riveted on the sandy beach. As much as she tried, she could not help but notice the dark shape in her peripheral vision and recognize it was easily keeping pace and moving in a lazy circle under their raft. *What the hell is that?* she wondered, not sure if she wanted to know. Suddenly, as if hearing her thoughts, the thing rose to the surface, and Jade turned to look. She could not believe her eyes. The head of the biggest crocodile she ever saw, even in the movies, broke the surface and stared at her.

Jade blinked. Her mind was unable to process the scene before her eyes. *I do not see this*, she thought as if she could wish the thing away. *This can't be happening.* As if obeying her command, the creature slowly sank back under the water until it was nothing but a large black mass moving beneath the surface again and was out of sight. Jade knew this was worse. *The damn thing could be anywhere.* Clearing her throat, Jade glanced over her shoulder at Sal who was working the raft's turbo rudder to keep them in the straightest line possible. "Um, Sal," she started. "I think we have a problem."

"Yep, saw that," Sal said goosing the turbo to get all she could get out of it. "Hang on. We're going to get to that beach but be ready because this raft will be coming to a sudden stop when it hits the sand."

Jade nodded, completely understanding her strategy. They had to get off the water, onto the beach, and into the jungle, before the giant crocodile could track them down.

"Take the duffel," Sal said pulling it off her shoulder and swinging it with one hand by the strap. Without waiting for confirmation, the woman threw it in Jade's direction. Almost out of self-defense, she caught it and slipped the shoulder strap across her body. It was ridiculously heavy, filled with everything Sal could stuff in it and Jade had a fleeting thought of how strong Sal was to carry it, the rifle, and Jade all at the same time while jumping out of the spaceship. Then, all thoughts were gone when Jade saw the most frightening thing she ever witnessed in all her years with the Space Rangers.

Behind the raft, a wake built and not only from the raft. Something was behind them, moving fast, right below the surface. "Sal, faster," Jade said, but the sound was not much more than a whisper. She watched Sal shake her head with frustration as she swung the rifle around her body to hold it with one hand while steering the boat. Just then, a crocodile as big as a school bus broke the surface, with its mouth wide and filled with yellow teeth. Unable to help herself, Jade screamed. Still, even as panic started to grip her, she watched Sal aim and unload a blast from the laser rifle right into the beast's mouth. The creature flailed, let out a screech of its own, and fell back with a huge splash.

As much as she liked seeing the thing disappear under the water again, Jade did not understand what happened. The thing's head should have disintegrated under the rifle's blast. "Are you on stun?" Jade asked, completely confused. It seemed impossible Sal would make that kind of mistake.

"Don't worry about it," Sal said, her jaw clenched.

"Are you kidding me?" Jade said. "The thing is trying to eat us."

"I said don't worry about it," Sal repeated, as she steered them to the beach. "But I strongly suggest you get ready to take a running leap." Switching her focus from the crocodile, Jade did as she was asked. The raft shot across the water hitting the sand and sliding about two yards before plowing in and doing precisely what Sal predicted. It came to a sudden stop. Jade felt herself hurdled head over heels, with the duffel bag smacking against her back until she came to a rolling stop. The breath was knocked out of her, sand filled her mouth, as well as a dozen other places, but before she could react, Sal was with her. The woman grabbed her by the back of her shirt to pull her upright while at a full run.

"Up!" she ordered. Jade scrambled to her feet letting Sal pull her into the thick wall of vegetation edging the beach. As they pushed through the giant leaves into the deep green jungle, she heard Sal muttering.

"What did you say?" Jade asked and without breaking stride, Sal responded.

"Next time I get to pick the fucking planet."

CHAPTER 17
NAT

While watching the Space Ranger cadets run the advanced-level obstacle course, Nat's mind wandered back to Sal. On the metro commute, she went back and forth over what Dee said to her and Catherine at the apartment. *Could it possibly be true?* she wondered. *Could Salishan Bransen have sunk so low?* If it were another member of the Space Rangers, the news would seem improbable, but for the ex-Space Ranger turn pirate, she would not bet on Sal's innocence. The woman's motivation was the question. *Why would Sal do such a thing? Or more likely, how would she benefit?*

As Nat watched a group of cadets come around a far corner of the obstacle course, she could not help but reflect on their youth. They were young and fast. *Unlike me*, she thought and shifted her weight from one leg to the next as the stiffness in her bionic knee reminded her that her days working out on obstacle courses were over. Nat frowned. This was the second time in one day she caught herself reflecting on the fact she was no longer Space Ranger quality. To be effective in the field, a Ranger must be one hundred percent ready and able all of the time or the lives of others were in danger. *So, will I spend the rest of my years in the corps as an instructor? Or should I simply retire?*

Deciding she needed to think of something else before the all too familiar depression set in, she let her mind return to Sal. Maybe while she was waiting for the next batch of cadets to reach her point in the course, she could check her commlink and see if there were any updates on Sal's status. Reaching into the pocket of her jacket, she realized she did not have the device and scanned her memory to think about where she saw it last. *Back at the apartment with Catherine*, she thought and knew she needed to make one hundred percent sure that was where the thing was since it was a secure device.

Seeing one of her fellow instructors jogging toward her as he followed the obstacle course checking for stragglers, she gave him a wave. "Sergeant, can you relieve me for five minutes?" she asked. "I need to make a quick trip into the training office."

"No problem, Captain," he said. "I can monitor activity using the hovercraft from here."

Nat smiled. "Appreciate that. I'll be right back," she said jogging across the grass in the direction of the training headquarters and ignoring the fact the sudden movement made a throbbing start in her knee. Not painful but a constant reminder. She knew she injured herself in the line of duty saving many lives in the process, so her disability was worth the struggle, but that did not make it less frustrating. *It is what it is*, she thought, reaching the building and going straight to her office. The computer was on, giving her the idea to take a quick look at the latest in the Salishan Bransen story while she called Catherine. As the commlink rang, Nat scrolled the screen and was surprised to find nothing about the president's assassination. Frowning, she only half heard the voice in her ear.

"Hello?" Catherine asked. "Nat, are you there?"

"Sorry," Nat said. "I was looking at something. Sweetheart, did I leave my commlink at the apartment?"

"You did," Catherine answered. "I'm almost to your building to bring it to you. I will be there in a few minutes."

Nat smiled. Catherine was not only young and beautiful, but she was thoughtful, and Nat appreciated it. "Thank you. I'll meet you in the lobby," Nat said. "Love you."

"I love you, too," Catherine responded, a smile in her voice. Then, the line clicked off, and Nat turned back to the computer. While she gave Catherine a few minutes before heading to the lobby to meet her, Nat scrolled the touchscreen a bit more to see if she could dig a little deeper. Going past the initial firewall, she finally saw some information about Salishan Bransen, but it was all marked top-secret. Nat grew even more curious. She understood because of the woman's background and her undercover work, that some of her files would be restricted, but the latest information regarding her alleged crime should have been easier to pull up. *After all, it was an all-points bulletin Dee relayed to us. Perhaps Sal's been apprehended?* Nat wondered. *But then why not advertise it and call off the manhunt?* After a few more inquiries into different files, again being blocked, Nat grew frustrated and was tempted to use her Catwoman login and password. She wondered if they were still active. Six months might be long enough to have them disabled. *Did they remember to shut down my super-secret access?* She tapped the desktop with a finger, contemplating what to do next. *What would it hurt to try?*

She was rewarded with a prompt which made her smile. "Hello Catwoman, long time no see," the female artificial intelligence voice said. *Nothing like a little AI to make you feel welcome*, Nat thought, happy to know her clearance was still in place. *As if maybe someday I can be a pilot again.* "How can I help you?"

"I'm looking for information as to the alleged assassination attempt of the president of the 8th Galaxy by ex-Space Ranger Salishan Bransen," Nat explained. "But I'm finding this is top-secret. Can you access the files?" There was a pause, and then a document popped up on the screen. Nat scanned it and saw in-depth details as to what Salishan had supposedly done. Nat was about to scroll down when the screen flipped to black. Frowning, she tapped the screen, but there was no response.

"AI?" she asked. "Are you still there?" There was no response. "AI, this is Catwoman requesting access," Nate repeated. The screen stayed blank. Furrowing her brow and wondering what to try next, she noticed the desk-set commlink was blinking. Nate saw the call was coming from the lobby. As she reached to press the button to acknowledge she was on her way down, a message popped up on the computer screen which made her catch her breath. In bold red letters was a warning she accessed restricted files considered top-secret.

"Remain in your location for agent interception," stated the last line of the message.

What the hell? Nate thought as she stood up slowly. Part of her wanted to follow the orders, but another part of her knew when something was up. If nothing else, she could explain later she was already on her way to the lobby before anything appeared on screen to tell her otherwise. One thing she did know, she was not going to wait around in the office to be interrogated about her relationship with Sal. That seemed like a poor career move.

Nat went to the elevators and noticed on the screen above the doors it was rising to her floor. *They could not possibly be reacting that quickly,* she thought but then decided to take the stairs, bad knee or no bad knee. Moving fast, she went to the stairwell door, slipped through, and closed it gently behind her as she heard the elevator doors bing their arrival and slide open. *Time to go.* Ignoring the hitch in her leg, she descended the ten stories and then busted into the lobby at a quick pace. Catherine waited for her in one of the chairs around the coffee table covered with tablets for light reading while people waited. Her girlfriend smiled when she saw her, but then it faltered when she noticed the look on Nat's face. Standing up as Nat reached her, questions were in her eyes, but Nat took her by the elbow, turning her toward the front doors. Their conversation would be better served outside than in the lobby where someone could overhear it. Something was going on, and she wanted to be as cautious as possible.

"Is everything okay?" Catherine asked. Nat rubbed her arm as she pushed through the exit.

"Of course," she said. "Thank you for bringing me my commlink. I just want some fresh air."

Catherine stopped, turning to look into Nat's face. "I know something is up," she said. "Don't treat me like I'm some fragile thing to be protected."

Nat frowned, not sure how to respond. Catherine was precisely those things to her, it was as simple as that, and right now, she was not sure what was coming next. Before she could respond, Catherine held up the commlink and pointed to a red icon on the screen.

"Nat, I don't know the exact situation, but I can tell you are concerned, and I believe it has something to do with this," she said. "There's a message on here, which I could not help but notice is addressed to Catwoman."

With a sigh, Nat took the device trying to decide if she should look at it now or maybe back in her office or even perhaps away from the academy altogether. Trying to make up her mind, she glanced back through the glass of the lobby doors in time to see two Ranger agents coming out of the elevator. They were looking for something. In her heart, Nat had no doubt they were the same ones who were on the elevator coming to her office. *To talk to me about inquiring online regarding Sal,* she thought.

"We need to go," Nat said hoping to get away before they spotted her. "Right now." Thankfully, Catherine did not hesitate when Nat led her across the parking lot toward the metro stop which fed into the Space Ranger Academy. She was not sure what she would do if there were no trains coming when they reached the platform, but hopefully being in a public place would deter the agents from making a scene. As they hustled down the escalator, she was happy Catherine was not asking questions. There would be time to discuss everything later, but right now they needed to get out of the area. Reaching the platform, Nat was relieved to hear the whooshing sound of an oncoming transport. With any luck, they would be on their way before the agents appeared.

The transport slowed at the same time Nat looked back at the escalators, only to realize the two agents from the lobby were racing down the steps. *Maybe I should handle this here on the platform?* Nat thought. *But first I need Catherine on the train and out of trouble.* As the transport stopped to hover in place, the doors slid open, and Nat hurriedly escorted Catherine onboard, only to turn to go back out again. Catherine grabbed her arm. "Where are you going?" she asked. Not wanting to say, but needing to know how close they were, Nat glanced over her shoulder and saw the agents were on the platform separating to flank her. Seeing the two men, she heard Catherine suck in a breath. "Are they here for us?" she asked.

Nat nodded. "I think so," she answered. "Stay behind me."

"But—" Catherine started as Nat turned to face the men rising on the balls of her feet in case they wanted to make things messy. A dozen people exited the train, walking across the platform, and Nat hoped that they would provide cover while she got Catherine away.

Nat felt Catherine grab her arm. "Get on here with me," Catherine insisted. "They can't do anything to us on the busy train." Nat considered what she said hearing the chime of the doors getting ready to close. Clenching her jaw, she hated the idea of running away rather than standing to fight, but Catherine was right. It was better to flee now. Backing up, Nat stepped inside the transport as the doors closed. The two agents sprinted toward them and almost made it, but were an instant too late. Nat gave a little wave at their frustrated faces as the transport started to move and slipped down the tunnel.

"Where we going?" Catherine asked, relief clear in her voice.

"Not back to the apartment," Nat said, pulling the comm-link from her pocket to look at the screen. The red icon was still there, and it was time to read the message. Encrypted text addressed to Catwoman was on the small screen. Like Catherine, she knew it could only be from Sal. She hesitated and wondered if she was doing the right thing by not going back and explaining the situation to her commander. Handing over the device with the message was what she would have done six months before. But now she hesitated. Nat owed Sal for rescuing Catherine. *But if the woman really has assassinated the president, does that not nullify everything?* she wondered.

Finally, she looked at Catherine and saw the pleading look in her eyes. Nat sighed. She needed to at least see what Sal sent her. Quickly, she held the link up to her eye for a retinal scan. After a second, a bizarre message popped up, yet she knew immediately what it meant. 173482-B11. It was a location code.

"What does it say?" Catherine asked, impatience in her voice.

"It's a location," she replied but was one she did not recognize, even though she was familiar with a lot of the galaxy. *Has she gone to some uncharted area?* she wondered. If so, that would require using hyperspace and possibly ending up at a batch of planets that were uninhabitable. *Would she do that?* Under the circumstances, with an APB out on her and pretty much the entire Space Ranger Corps searching, Nat realized she probably would.

"We should go there," Catherine said. Nat furrowed her brow and knew she had a heck of a decision to make.

CHAPTER 18
CATHERINE

Catherine knew the last thing to do was try talking Nat into to helping Sal. There were many things Catherine loved about her tall, confident girlfriend, but the woman's stubborn streak was tricky. Even after six months, Catherine knew Nat only came to a decision on her own. Otherwise, she would not go along with it. *Especially if it means going against the Space Ranger Corps,* she thought knowing helping Sal, who was apparently wanted across the galaxy, would definitely be illegal. *And dangerous.* Finally, Nat puffed out a frustrated breath and clicked the commlink off. She slipped it into her pocket and looked at Catherine. Catherine held perfectly still while she waited for the woman's decision. *Please let her be willing to help Sal.*

"All right, but I need to know at least a little more information," Nat said, and Catherine felt a huge sense of relief. At least Nat was willing to consider helping Sal. "First, I want to get ahold of Dee, so I need a secure link." Just then, Catherine saw the woman's face turn hard while she looked over Catherine's shoulder. Turning to follow her gaze, Catherine saw the two agents who were on the platform as the train was about to leave.

"How?" Catherine asked, not able to get out more words. They were about to be captured, the commlink would be seized, and who knew what would happen to Sal.

Nat shook her head. "Somehow they must've gotten on the train at the back as it was moving away," she said. Not sure what to do, Catherine turned back to Nat as she took her elbow, starting to pull her behind her for protection. Realizing Nat was preparing to fight the two men, Catherine knew she needed to do something. Although she saw her lover fight space pirates, and knew Nat was strong and skilled in hand-to-hand combat, she also could see the two agents coming toward them were armed. Nat was not. They needed to run.

A glance around the car did not help. There were only two other people in their compartment, and one looked asleep. The transport emerged from the tunnel at another stop and Catherine prayed the doors would open before the men reached them. "Nat, we can't fight them here," she said, pulling away. "They have weapons. We need to go." As if they could hear her, Catherine watched the men speed up, racing down the length of the last car next to theirs. As they started through the connector, the transport halted, and after what felt like forever, the doors to their car slid open.

"Go!" Nat said, grabbing her hand. They dodged people as they ran across the platform, heading toward the escalators. Catherine was thankful this was a busy stop, and people crowded the space. It was the cover they needed.

"Halt," one the agent's yelled. *That is the last thing we're going to do,* Catherine thought as they reached the escalator and took the steps two by two. Blasting out of the stairwell, Catherine followed Nat through the honking traffic of a menagerie of surface spacecraft as she raced across the multilane street toward a strip mall. Again, Catherine heard one of the men yell behind them, but at that moment, Nat hurried her down the alleyway between two buildings. They came out behind the mall. "Shit," she heard Nat mutter and looking around, Catherine saw the problem. There was almost nothing to hide behind. Only a set of green dumpsters.

"What about those?" she asked pointing at the metal containers.

Nat gave them one look and shook her head. "The first place they'll look," she answered. Catherine watched the woman turn in every direction trying to figure out what to do. Suddenly, Catherine had an idea. She hated to think of Nat facing the two men, but it was going to happen one way or another. At least her option gave Nat an advantage.

"I've thought of something," Catherine said as she led Nat to the dumpsters. "I'll get inside of one of these and make noise so that they think we are in there."

A look of understanding crossed Nat's face. "But I'll be hiding," she said. "And when they are distracted, hit them from behind."

Catherine nodded, watching Nat open the lid. She paused as the stink of garbage wafted out. "Catherine, I can't ask—" she started, but Catherine stepped up to the edge. This was not a time to be dainty.

"I'll need a boost," she said, and without another word, Nat helped her get inside among the trash.

"I love you," Nat said. and Catherine wished there was more time to tell Nat everything in her heart. *Please don't let anything happen to her*, she thought but smiled through her fear.

"Be careful," Catherine said. "And kick their asses." Nat nodded and then she closed the lid. The space became nearly pitch black, with only the smallest sliver of light coming in around the top. With no idea what she was stepping on, Catherine started to shift around in the dumpster making it clear someone was inside. It was a desperate plan, but she refused to let herself think it would not work. Nat's safety, and Sal's too, depended on it.

Not more than a minute passed when Catherine heard the sound of footsteps on the pavement. She was sure at any moment the lid would open, and they would find her. *I need a weapon*, she thought, gritting her teeth as she felt around in the trash for anything useable. Shifting through nothing but a soggy mess, she froze when the lid of the trash bin started to shake. *This is it.* With no more time, she raised her fists, ready to punch any face who peeked in.

Suddenly, she heard a loud thud outside the dumpster and whoever was trying to open the lid was no longer focused on it. She heard a man yell and then another thump as if somebody hit the ground. There were a couple more smacking sounds until all was quiet but for a groan. Catherine hated not knowing what was happening. *Do I look? What if the groan was Nat?* she worried. She needed to look. Peeking out, what she saw made her heart stop. Even though one of the agents was down on the ground and unconscious, the other one had Nat in a headlock from behind. The woman was wrestling him with one hand, trying to break his hold, while grasping his wrist with her other. Catherine realized Nat was trying to stop him from pointing his weapon at her. There was no doubt in Catherine's mind, Nat was losing the fight. She had to do something.

Knowing she did not have time to climb out of the dumpster, she went with what was readily available. Reaching into the stinking pile of garbage all around her, she grabbed the first soft mess she felt. Fleetingly hoping it was a full diaper she now held in her hand, Catherine aimed for the back of the man's head and threw with all her strength. The throw could never have been better.

She heard the splat as the stinking package struck the agent. The attack was such a surprise, the agent froze for a nanosecond. It was all Nat needed. With the man's arm around her neck, making him bend a little at the waist, Nat pushed her hip into his side. She flung him over her head in a perfectly executed move. The man landed hard on his back, and before he could even react, Nat dropped a knee onto his neck, grabbing his plasma gun. She held it to his forehead. The man froze.

"I have one question for you," Catherine heard Nat say with the growl. "Why does anyone care if I was researching Salishan Bransen?" The man clamped his jaw shut, and Catherine could tell he was not going to respond. She heard Nat puff out a frustrated breath. "So, you are willing to die over this?"

"Nat, wait," Catherine said. "What if he doesn't know anything?

Nat paused, her face thoughtful, while the agent's eyes glared up at her. Finally, Nat shook her head. "Unfortunately, I think you are right," she said and then Catherine watched her turn the weapon to stun, step back quickly and fire at the man's chest. From such close range, the shock nearly lifted the man off of the ground, but it did not kill him.

Stuffing the gun into the waistband of her pants, Nat came back to the dumpster and easily lifted Catherine out. "Now what?" Catherine asked as Nat pulled her into a hug. They held each other for a moment, and Catherine could hear her lover's racing heart. "I'm okay," Catherine assured her. "You kept me safe." Finally, Nat let go and looked into Catherine's face.

"I won't be able to stand it if anything happens to you," she said. Catherine smiled to reassure her, getting up onto tiptoe to give Nat a quick kiss.

"I know," she said. "You are my hero." She felt Nat relax with those words, refocusing on the situation at hand.

"We need to find a place to hole up," she said, taking Catherine's hand and leading her back out of the alley to the street. "And get a throwaway commlink so I can call Dee. I have to know what we are dealing with." Catherine could not agree more.

CHAPTER 19
SAL

Sal and Jade hiked through the jungle. It was slow going navigating around giant leafed bushes, and vines as thick as Sal's arm dangling from trees all around them, even an occasional bog of quicksand. The trek was exhausting work, and even though Sal would never admit the truth, after hours of struggling without even a shadow of a trail, she was a little winded. Glancing back from time to time, she noted Jade was doing a decent job of keeping up. The woman was in excellent physical shape, something Sal noticed on more than one occasion. *Call it what it is,* she thought. *Her body is sexy as hell.* Still, that did not necessarily translate to endurance. *Apparently, the beautiful Miss Hamilton has spent some time on jogging trails.* Sal smirked at the idea of how such endurance could come in handy later.

As they broke from under the canopy of trees into an open expanse of tall grass, Jade called for a stop. "Where exactly are we going?" she asked, her breathing coming in gasps. "We've been walking for hours."

"There," Sal said, pointing up over the trees to a butte still miles in the distance. "I saw it from the lake right before we crashed."

Jade shook her head. "And why are we bothering to climb that?" she asked, her tone taking on a bit of frustration. "I thought we were searching for some sort of settlement." Sal tilted her head, studying Jade for a moment. The woman was willing to walk for half the day without asking any questions, possibly so grateful she didn't drown that she was cooperative. *Suddenly, she wants to know the plan?* Sal wondered. *Well, now she knows.*

With a shrug, Sal turned back around to keep walking. "Nope," she said. "Just planning to get up high enough to see what's around here." The butte was the highest elevation anywhere in the area and would give them an excellent vantage point to look around. She hoped to see something or someplace where they could get their hands on a spaceship. Sal held no qualms about stealing one, whether through stealth or firepower. The last thing she intended was to remain a sitting duck on this jungle planet in case the Rangers were able to intercept her last transmission to Catwoman. *Or if Nat turns me in*, she thought. Trusting the Space Ranger was based solely on gut instinct, and for Sal, it was rarely wrong. *Still, there was no one in the universe with more honor than Nat. The question was how that translated in Nat's mind.*

Knowing she could do nothing about it now, Sal walked another twenty yards when she realized Jade was not following. Sal glanced back to see the woman staring up at the sky. With her face flushed from exertion and sweat plastering her t-shirt to her body, Sal felt a twist of attraction. *Maybe when this is all over* ... she thought as Jade dropped her eyes to Sal's. The chemistry which was always there sizzled, and the woman bit her lip, but a boldness lingered in her eyes. *Definitely could be time to find a place to stop.*

"No," Jade said as if reading Sal's mind.

Sal raised an eyebrow. "No, what?" she asked.

Jade walked closer to stop in front of Sal. She put her hands on her hips. "No, I'm not walking to the big pile of rocks," she replied.

Sal narrowed her eyes, unsure if Jade meant not now, or not ever. It had been hours of pushing through the rugged terrain, and they would not make the butte before nightfall. Being out in the open when darkness fell was not high on Sal's list of fun activities either. So far, they had not encountered any predators, but Sal knew they were out there. After seeing the giant crocodile in the lake, Sal wondered if they landed onto some under-evolved planet. *Which means about anything could be running around here, including things with very big, very sharp teeth.*

"We can take a break," Sal said, dropping the duffle bag she carried. "But not long. It will get too dark to move around once the sun goes down." She pulled a flask of water from the bag and took a long pull before holding it out to Jade. The woman took the bottle without breaking eye contact. After a beat, she took a deep drink of her own, then closed her eyes and sighed from the refreshment.

Seeing the woman was feeling better already, Sal grabbed the bag, crossed the strap over her body, and prepared to walk again. "Hold it," Jade said. "I think you've forgotten something."

Sal paused. "Like what exactly?" she asked, already know-ing she was not going to like the answer.

"That I'm in charge of this mission," Jade said. She was en-tirely serious, and Sal barked out a laugh.

"Screw that," she said. "You stopped being in charge about the time I climbed up the damn cable into the starship. Now, let's go. Daylight's fading and I have a strong sense there will be plenty around here ready to make a bump in the night." As if in answer, there was a sudden roar from the jungle not far into the trees across from them. A shriek of an animal in pain followed. *That sounded big*, Sal thought and felt Jade come up beside her.

"What was that?" she whispered.

Sal shook her head. "Not sure, not wanting to find out," she said. "Maybe we have traveled far enough for today. What do you say we find a nice tall tree with broad branches for us to climb? Rather not be on the ground when it's dark. How about you?"

Jade shook her head. "No," she agreed. "I haven't done as much fieldwork as you have, but I did pay attention in class at the academy. The first rule of jungle planets is never get caught on the ground at night."

"Good rule," Sal said scanning the tree line around the clearing. One tree stood out above the rest. "How about that monster of a tree over there?" It was one of the tallest around, and its branches ran for easily twenty yards in every direction. A couple of them looked as wide as the hallway down the mid-dle of a carrier ship. *As long as we don't walk in our sleep, it will work perfectly*, she thought.

Jade followed her gaze, relieved when she saw where Sal in-tended. "Perfect," she said and this time did not hesitate when

Sal started walking. As they made their way back into the tropical foliage and to the base of the tree, Sal saw a flicker of movement to her right. Dropping to a crouch, she pulled the plasma gun in one smooth motion only to see nothing amongst the leaves. She was pleased to note Jade followed her lead and dropped down without a word. They both stayed frozen and waited, but there was no more movement.

Not until Sal stood back up did Jade make a sound. "What did you see?" Jade asked, and Sal shook her head.

"Not sure," she answered. Holstering the weapon, she turned back to look at the trunk of the gigantic tree. "I thought I saw something moving."

"Something big?" Jade asked, and Sal shrugged as she grabbed a thick vine running around the trunk, preparing to climb.

"I couldn't tell," she replied. "It was moving fast." With that, she pulled herself up a few feet and began to make her ascent. After she had gone about ten meters, she looked down to see if Jade was following. The woman was right beneath her, and again Sal was impressed with the woman's strength and skill. *Stubborn and bossy, but not just a pretty face*, she thought and knew if she said something like that to Jade, she would be pissed. *Just another thing I like about her.*

As they made their way up the trunk to the lowest branches, Sal stopped to look down and was surprised to realize they were at least ten stories up already. Again, she hoped neither of them tossed and turned in the night or it would be a rude awakening when they landed. *But ideally, this will keep any of the bed bugs from biting tonight*, she thought as she crested the broad branch and stood up. Turning back, she held out a hand to help Jade the last little bit. The woman ignored her and made it the rest of the way on her own.

Sal could not help but snort a laugh. It was not often a woman surprised her, but Jade was starting to more often than not. Things with this woman were never what they appeared. "What's so funny?" Jade asked once she was standing.

Shaking her head, Sal did not bother to explain and instead looked at the tree. She was pleased to see a hole at the spot where the branch left the trunk. Big enough for two people, but barely. Cozy quarters, but both of them could duck into it for the night and be less likely to slip off the branch in the dark. "Well," Sal said, lifting her chin toward the hollow opening. "Home, sweet, home?"

She watched Jade follow her stare and then smile. "Not the Royal Venus Hotel," Jade said. "But under the circumstances, I think we got off lucky."

Then, Sal saw something growing on the side of the trunk "This night just got a whole lot better," she said, moving toward the object laced up in the bark.

"What is it?" Jade said, coming to look.

Sal reached for her knife and pried off a bit of fungus. Sniffing it, Sal grinned. "Yes, a good night indeed," she said.

"What is that?" Jade asked again.

Sal turned and gave her a wink. "It's called Angel's Fire," she answered. "Or at least that's what we called it in the space pirates. A little something to snack on." Jade raised her eyebrows and Sal was pleased she did not immediately question what Sal was insinuating.

"Angel's Fire does not sound like a normal appetizer," Jade remarked.

"Oh, most definitely not," Sal said as she put some in the side pocket of the duffel bag. "Once we get settled, maybe I'll show you what this stuff can do. If you're open to trying new things?" Sal let the insinuation hang between them and was again pleased when Jade did not immediately turn her down. It might be a jungle planet, and the humidity was high, but once night fell, it would get a little cooler. In Sal's experience, there was nothing wrong with snuggling with the sexy woman to keep warm in the night.

CHAPTER 20
NAT

Nat paced the dive of a hotel room and tried not to let her thoughts get carried away. *What if something happened to Dee because of the encrypted message I sent her?* she wondered. It seemed unlikely whoever was hot on their trail would have deduced she would reach out to her friend, but then nothing seemed logical at the moment. While she continued to move restlessly from wall to wall, Catherine sat quietly on the foot of the bed. Nat could tell by the look in her eyes she was worried, no doubt about Dee, but especially Sal. Nat accepted the fact her girlfriend held a special connection to the ex-Space Ranger. For a while, she worried there was something intimate between them, but over time, as her love with Catherine grew stronger, she changed her mind. There was specialness there, but not romantic love.

If she was honest with herself, Nat had a unique connection with Sal too. Hers was based more on gratitude than anything. After all, the woman saved them once, helping them escape from the space pirate hideaway. *But is it enough that I am willing to risk everything to help her?* Nat wondered as she glanced at the throwaway commlink on the battered old nightstand and waited for Dee's call. Puffing out a frustrated breath, she willed the thing to buzz.

"Maybe we should find something to eat?" Catherine suggested. "While we wait?"

Running a hand over her face, Nat considered the idea. *A watched pot never boils*, she thought and started to agree when the commlink finally chimed. Snatching it up, she pressed the button to connect. Before she said hello or identified herself, Dee was talking.

"Please tell me this does not have anything to do with what I think it has to do with," she said. "Because if it is, I'm going to hang up right now."

"Wait," Nat said. "Let's say it may very well be what we talked about before, but things have escalated, and I need answers."

There was a pause, and Nat heard a sigh of frustration over the line. "There is only one answer you need," Dee said. "It is to stay well clear of this mess. Your name has already popped up in connection with what we are not talking about."

"It has?" Nat asked feeling a tightness in her chest from the anxiety of being associated with the assassination of the president of the 8th Galaxy.

"Not like accomplices," Dee said. "But certainly as a person of interest."

Nat closed her eyes and tried to refrain from punching the wall. "Shit," Nat said. "Then, I need more information. Because if I'm going to get sucked into this, I need to know details."

"I can't help you," Dee said. "And it's not because I won't, because you have saved my ass multiple times throughout our careers, but I simply don't have anything."

Nat thought of the encrypted message. "So, no one knows where she is?" she asked.

"Not that I've heard or seen," Dee answered. "She seems to have vanished. But then, this is you know who, so I'm not surprised."

Nat nodded. Sal had incredible skills in about every area of espionage and survival. Still, it could be a ruse. "Are you sure?" Nat asked. "Or is that only the cover story."

"No," Dee replied with certainty in her voice. "I am confident this one piece of information is accurate. People are scrambling to try to find her. And now you."

"Okay," Nat said not at all happy to know her name was now on the APB. "I will lay low until I hear from you again." There was a long pause before Dee responded.

"Nat," she said. "You are my friend and always will be, but don't do anything stupid. This is not your problem."

"I hear you," Nat replied, although she could not honestly answer what she was going to do next. "Catwoman signing off." Once disconnected, Nat put the device on the nightstand and looked at Catherine. The woman's eyes were scanning her face, and Nat knew she was trying to read what Nat would do next. *If only I knew*, she thought and slipped onto the edge of the bed beside Catherine. She took the woman's hand and looked at their interlaced fingers. Going after Sal would put them in danger, yet, she knew Catherine wanted to help Sal no matter the cost. *It will mean getting my hands on a starship too*, she thought, not sure how she could make that happen. "You want this, don't you?" Nat asked barely loud enough for Catherine to hear her and the woman gave her a slow nod.

"I do," she replied. "Because I know she would do it for us."

Nat paused considering what Catherine said. It was true. Somehow, she knew Sal would do whatever it took to help them if it came down to it. *Hadn't she proven that already?* Nat thought suddenly feeling a renewed sense of purpose. She would find the ex-Space Ranger. *And once I do, then I can decide what to do with her.* Nat nodded. "You're right," she agreed. "Let's go find her."

Before she knew it, Catherine's arms were around her neck, and her mouth was on Nat's. Suddenly, Nat felt more alive than she had in months. The idea an adventure was right in front of her filled her with excitement, and Catherine's lips on hers made desire well up from her core. Running her hands along Catherine's hips and encircling her waist, she pulled the woman onto her lap without breaking the kiss. She felt Catherine moan into her mouth and in an instant, Nat wanted nothing more than to have Catherine naked and under her on the bed.

Feeling her need, Catherine ran her hands up the front of Nat's shirt and started to pull at the buttons of her uniform. Even though her movement bordered on frantic, it was not fast enough for Nat, and she broke the kiss to pull the fabric off over her head, leaving her in nothing but her sports bra. For a moment, Catherine paused as she ran her eyes along the muscles of Nat's shoulders. There was a look of hunger in the younger woman's eyes. "Do you want me?" she asked, and Nat smiled. There was never a time since she saw Catherine she did not want the woman, but lately, she had not felt complete. She was not the mighty Space Ranger she used to be when Catherine first met her. But now, all of that confidence was back and, as her heart pounded, she wanted nothing but to touch Catherine until she cried out her name.

Taking Catherine in her arms, Nat stood, lifting the smaller woman easily, switching their positions. "What are you doing?" Catherine gasped, but Nat did not answer. She was not interested in words. Not right now. This was a time for action, and as she laid Catherine down, she slid her hands between the woman's legs and parted them. She was pleased when Catherine instinctively lifted her hips to greet Nat moving in against her. With a growl, Nat reached for the buttons to unfasten Catherine's pants, while the woman kicked off her sandals.

"I want to taste you," Nat said, noting the passion in Catherine's half-closed eyes. Catherine licked her lips, and Nat knew her lover was wet already. As a wave of heat rolled over her, Nat slipped the clothing off her lover's hips and leaned over to kiss the soft skin above the hair between Catherine's legs. Feeling the woman shiver with excitement, Nat smiled. Although every part of her screamed to let go and ravish Catherine, she also knew making her wait to come would heighten the pleasure for them both.

Slowing down, Nat moved her thumbs under the waistband of Catherine's pants and stepping back, pulled the clothing off of her in a single, swift movement. All that remained was a pair of white lace panties, and Nat raised an eyebrow. They looked very much like the first pair of Catherine's she ever touched. So much had changed since then, and what was once a confusing relationship between them was nothing but passion, trust, and most definitely love. *I love her more than anything in the world*, Nat thought. *And if risking everything to save Sal is what it takes to show her, then I will find the woman.*

Noticing her pause, Catherine lifted her head with a hint of a smile. "Nat?" she asked, and their eyes met. As if seeing all of Nat's emotions on her face, Catherine held out her arms. "Come here." Nat moved to her and slipped into the embrace. As she nuzzled her face into Catherine's neck, she felt the woman's mouth whisper against her ear. "I want to feel you inside me," she said. "I want to feel all your strength as you take me." Nat sucked in a breath. No one ever made her feel as powerful as Catherine.

"Are you sure?" Nat asked. "I don't want to hurt you, but I don't know if I can control myself." In answer, Catherine took one of Nat's hands and moved it down her body until it was between her legs. Nat felt the heat of the woman's swollen lips against her fingertips. Unable to deny the invitation, she slipped her fingers inside Catherine, hearing her gasp at suddenly being so full.

"Oh, baby," she moaned and started to move her hips. "You feel so good." Matching her rhythm, Nat started to stroke in and out, building up faster and faster. Every thrust was deeper than the one before. It had been months since she made love to Catherine with such intensity and Nat felt the return of her power.

"Do you want more?" Nat growled into Catherine's ear, and the woman started to whimper.

"Yes," she answered, her voice breathless.

"Yes, what?" Nat asked needing to hear Catherine submit to her completely.

"Please, yes," Catherine answered, and Nat rewarded her with the deepest thrust of all. It was enough, and Catherine cried out while her body clenched around Nat's hand. With a scream, Catherine came, and Nat knew she was a powerful Space Ranger once more.

CHAPTER 21
JADE

It was going to be impossible for Jade and Sal not to touch each other all night in the close confines of the hollowed-out space in the giant tree. Even pulling her feet back and resting her chin on her knees while she sat on the floor, their shoulders were only a foot apart. Part of it was because Sal was so tall and broad-shouldered. Jade did not consider herself a petite woman by any standard, and not too many women or even men towered over her, but Sal seemed able to do that. *But is it because of her giant presence rather than her actual stature?* Jade wondered. There was never an instance where Jade thought the phrase "larger than life" was more appropriate than when describing Salishan Bransen.

"You're staring," Jade heard Sal say and it made her jump when she realized she was caught doing exactly that. *I'm certain I'm not the first woman to be captivated by this ex-space ranger*, she thought. She still felt herself blush, especially when a smirk played across Sal's face.

"I was wondering if there is anything in that duffel bag to eat," Jade said hoping to cover the attraction she knew was evident on her face.

Sal shrugged. "Help yourself," she said nudging the bag closer toward Jade. "I imagine there are emergency rations of some kind in there, although I can't promise they will taste good."

"I can deal," Jade said not liking the implication she was not adept enough at survival to look past bad tasting rations. "Nothing like a little dehydrated space food to fill our bellies." Jade reached for the strap and pulled the bulky bag onto her lap. The space inside the tree was even tighter, but she refrained from sliding closer to Sal.

Opening the zipper, she looked inside and found a couple of foil packets marked as edible. She held one up for Sal, but the woman shook her head. Instead, she pulled the knife from her belt and began to whittle slivers from the mushroom she plucked off the bark of the tree.

"No thanks," Sal said with a shake of her head. "These are better on an empty stomach."

Jade frowned. "Do you want to explain those to me a little more?" Jade asked. "Particularly, before you eat one."

Sal chuckled. "I told you already. This is called Angel's Fire, and it makes you relax."

"Relax?" Jade asked.

Sal raised an eyebrow and gave her a sly smile. "Exactly," she said. "Relax. And frankly, since we have nothing else to do at the moment, chilling out is a perfect option." Then her eyes shifted and met Jade's. There was a hint of something in them which made Jade's stomach tighten.

Is that desire? Jade wondered. *Why do I suddenly feel like I'm prey?* Involuntarily licking her lips, Jade held perfectly still as she waited to see what Sal would do next. After a beat, still keeping eye contact, Sal lifted a tiny piece of the mushroom with her blade and popped it into her mouth. Swallowing at the same time she sliced off another small chunk, she held it out on the tip of the knife for Jade.

Jade stared at it, not sure what to do. She never heard of this sort of fungus and wondered if Angel's Fire was the correct name for it. She did not put much stock in space pirate knowledge of flora or fauna. Still, she trusted Sal and did not believe the woman would put them in jeopardy. *And relaxing would be nice*, she thought. Taking a deep breath, Jade decided to throw caution to the wind and reached for the bit of spongy, brown substance. Before her hand touched it, Sal pulled back.

"Don't get it on your fingers if you don't have to," she said. "It works better if you don't disturb the spores on it. That's the part that works the best."

Jade looked into her eyes again and saw Sal was sincere. Again, putting her trust in the woman, Jade opened her mouth and waited. Slowly, Sal moved the blade closer and slipped the treat onto Jade's tongue. A tingle ran through Jade. For some reason, Sal's motion seemed incredibly intimate. *And arousing*, she thought. Only then she wondered if the wild delectable was like other psychedelic drugs and lowered inhibitions. *Because if it does, I don't know what will happen next.*

As she watched, Sal closed her eyes and leaned back against the side of the small space. Jade suddenly wanted their inhibitions to lower. *What if this gives me an opportunity to ask questions of Sal?* she wondered, excited at the prospect. There was much about the woman she wanted to know, or in a way, needed to know. *So many things I want her to admit to.* So far, there was no way to get the dark, moody stranger to open up and share. All Jade knew about Sal was what she read in her file. Even though it was thorough about her career, there was almost nothing about Sal as a person or about her time with the space pirates.

Feeling the effects of the Angel's Fire as her body relaxed and her mind spun free, she decided this might be her best chance to extract information. Hopefully, Sal was feeling the same. Jade cleared her throat and waited to see if Sal would respond. She was rewarded with the slightest shift of Sal's head and a look through narrowed eyes. "What?" Sal asked.

Jade paused. *What should I ask first?* she wondered, knowing even if under the influence, Sal would not easily be tricked into talking. "Why didn't you shoot to kill with the beast in the lake?" she finally asked. Sal blinked, then turned away again and closed her eyes. The two of them sat in silence, and Jade was about to lean back herself and close her eyes, suddenly being willing to let go of any thought of asking more questions. As Jade started to drift, she heard Sal speak.

"That creature is probably a couple of centuries old, and we are the ones invading his territory," Sal said, still sitting back with her eyes closed. "It is a mighty, majestic predator who rules his part of the lake. I was not going to destroy him unless my life depended on it."

Jade was thoughtful for a moment as she considered what Sal said. It was true killing the animal if they did not need to would have been a waste. Still, in the moment, Jade had been terrified. Killing the crocodile would have been fine with her. She was glad Sal made the right choice. *Interesting though, that Sal puts such store in the creatures of the wild and not so much in her kind*, Jade thought. She tilted her head to study Sal. *Could there be some compassion there after all?* Jade decided to probe deeper. She studied Sal's face, the chiseled lines, handsome features. *So attractive ...* Jade shook herself, realizing the drug was making her feel things she did not necessarily want to experience right now. She could not get distracted. The answers she wanted might be in her reach.

"So, did you have a pet when you were a child?" Jade asked. Again, it appeared Sal would not take the bait, but after a beat, she shook her head.

"Nope," Sal answered with eyes still closed. "Moved around too much." When she did not elaborate, Jade tried not to let her frustration show. She had interrogated dozens of suspects. Sal was a challenge, but not necessarily impossible. She was determined to pry loose some of the woman's secrets.

"I see," Jade said, deciding to try a sweeter approach. She slipped a little closer to Sal until their bodies were almost touching. "So why is that?" This time Sal snapped her head forward and regarded Jade with an intense look. Jade sucked in a breath in response to the coolness in the woman's eyes. Clearly, Jade already pushed the boundaries of where Sal wanted to go. *Over asking about a pet?* she wondered.

"Why are you asking me questions?" Sal asked. "Don't you know enough from my file?"

Jade raised an eyebrow deciding to press on even under Sal's stare. "Because I want to know more about the real you," she replied, leaning in closer so that her face was within an inch of Sal's. "Can't someone get to know you?"

Sal did not pull back and instead closed the distance even more until Jade could feel the woman's hot breath on her lips. *She's going to kiss me*, she thought feeling her pulse pounding throughout her body. Particularly between her legs. *Is it from the Angel's Fire or being this close to Sal?* Jade did not know, but her entire body was thrumming with arousal. Suddenly, she wanted nothing more than for Sal to have sex with her right there on the floor.

As if reading her mind, she saw Sal swallow. It was the only giveaway the woman felt any emotion. The rest of her face was like stone, and her eyes were cold. "Trust me," Sal whispered. "There is nothing about me you really want to know."

Jade would not give up. Not now. "I don't believe that," Jade said, her voice husky with desire. "I know there's more inside you. Let me see it."

With that, Sal closed the small distance between them and took Jade's mouth, firm and hot, with her own. Melting into the kiss, Jade felt consumed by the powerful aura of the woman. She opened her lips to accept Sal's tongue, which claimed her mouth with so much passion, Jade moaned. Although she had other lovers, she always considered herself the aggressor but not with Sal. With this woman, she simply wanted to give her whatever she desired.

Then, as quickly as it began, it was over. Sal pulled back, and when Jade opened her eyes, she saw humor replaced the coldness in the woman's demeanor. It was as if Sal was mocking her desire and suddenly Jade was furious. No doubt seeing the anger in Jade's face, Sal raised her eyebrows. "What?" she asked, with the hint of a laugh. "Did you think you could throw yourself at my head and unlock all my secrets?"

Jade did not bother to answer. Not only because she was angry at both the woman and herself, but because what Sal insinuated was true. That was what she was trying to do. *This is not over*, she thought as she scooted back to her place along the wall and settled in to stay there the rest of the night. *I will unlock you, Sal Bransen. I will get my answers, one way or another.*

CHAPTER 22
CATHERINE

As she slowly awoke, Catherine kept her eyes closed. She snuggled up to her woman, loving the comfort she felt in the broad shoulder where she rested her head. A smile played across her face as she remembered their lovemaking the night before. First the bed, and later in their favorite place—the shower. The vivid image of Nat on her knees as the hot water cascaded over both of them slipped into Catherine's mind. She felt her nipples tighten at the memory of Nat taking them into her mouth. The tug as the woman sucked one and then the other.

Squirming a little, Catherine felt her body tightening again at the thought. Nat tracing her tongue down Catherine's body, following a rivulet of water from the shower and until she was positioned right at Catherine's center. Catherine sucked in a deep breath remembering the moment.

"What could you possibly be thinking about to make that sound?" Nat asked. Catherine let out a giggle as she opened her eyes.

"Just remembering getting clean with you," she replied.

Nat chuckled and pulled Catherine closer. "Really?" Nat said. "Do I need to do something to help with that?"

Catherine giggled. "Captain Nat, you can't possibly want more of me already," she said. "Besides, we have a friend to save."

Nat answered by pulling her close and planting a kiss on her forehead. Catherine felt a different kind of stirring at her lover's tender embrace. Catherine loved their intimate moments most of all. She rested her head on Nat's shoulder and played her fingers along the skin of Nat's chest. She was thankful she had found this woman, even though they were hiding out in a dive of a hotel and the future was uncertain.

"So, what next?" Catherine asked, and she felt Nat let out a deep breath.

"Well," Nat started. "If we are going to do this, we need a spaceship to get there. Unfortunately, I don't know how we're going to pull that off."

Catherine understood. She had no idea how they would manage that either considering they were now on the run and with no access to funds. Then, the memory of her last adventure of finding a spaceship when she needed one came to mind. "Wait," she said, sitting up. "I might know where we can get one." She smiled at the woman's puzzled expression.

"Where?" Nat asked with a curious smile of her own. "Is there a rich uncle I don't know about?

Catherine shook her head. "No," she said with a laugh. "I was thinking about when I purchased the ED-90 so I could fly to Untas. Do you remember it?"

The humor left Nat's face, and Catherine knew she was recalling the close encounter she had when Catherine crashed the spaceship on the ice planet Taswa. Nat risked everything going to save her, and if she had not, Catherine would not be alive. The accident happened because she was driving that poor excuse of a spaceship. *And I bought it from a sleazy spaceship salesman who took advantage of my lack of experience*, she thought. "Well, it all ended fine," Catherine said to Nat reassuringly.

Nat touched Catherine's face with her fingertips, and a look of tenderness came into the strong woman's eyes. "Yes, it all turned out well for me, indeed," she said. "But if I ever get my hands on the man who sold you that hunk of junk.

"And that's my idea," Catherine explained. "I could take you to the lot where he set up. I think he travels from place to place, and we might get lucky. Maybe he's on his rotation to be there right now."

WHEN THEY ARRIVED AT the location Catherine remembered from her unpleasant experience, she saw they were in luck. In the worst part of town, they stopped at a large open asphalt lot with a small single-wide trailer, which knew better days, at the center. As soon as they got out of the Uberlift and started walking toward the menagerie of spaceships available, a man in an ugly brown suit and with an even worse combover came waddling toward them. His smile was broad and full of possibilities, with a twinkle in his eye, which Catherine knew disarmed would-be buyers. *Which is why he makes an excellent used spaceship salesman*, Catherine thought. As the man reached them, Nat stepped in front of Catherine so that she was not quite visible to the man. She assumed it was both to keep him from recognizing her before they had a chance to get the advantage, but also because it was her protective nature.

"Girls, girls," the salesman said as he neared them, his beefy hand outstretched. "So happy to have you here. You're in time for the sale of the century."

Catherine saw Nat glance down at the man's gesture. Undoubtedly, he was expecting a handshake. When the Space Ranger who towered over him did not respond in turn, she watched the man's smile falter for a moment. He dropped his hand and rubbed it on his pant leg. "I'm here to talk to you about a different matter," Nat said with steel in her voice. The man's mouth truly did start to sag. Wariness replaced the twinkle in his eye.

"What's that exactly?" he asked, his tone switching from jolly to irritated in the blink of an eye.

Nat moved a little to the left and put her hand on the small of Catherine's back. "It seems not too long ago you took advantage of a young woman's inexperience with spaceships and sold her a hunk of junk."

Catherine watched the salesman flick his eyes to her and study her face. There was no hint of recognition, and she realized he probably took advantage of so many different people that she did not stand out.

"About six months ago? An ED-90?" Catherine offered to help refresh his memory. "I paid in credits?" Then she watched as a look of recognition crossed his features. He even took a step back.

"I don't know what you are talking about," the man lied. "I assure you, I get everything in writing, and I do not take advantage of customers. Especially pretty young girls."

"Well," Nat started. "I found that not to be the case. The ED-90 you sold her at an inflated price was so unreliable it nearly cost her life."

The man licked his lips, and Catherine watched as he ran through his options. "I see," the man said. "But like I already told you, that is not something I would take responsibility for. I have all my spaceships checked before I put them up for sale to make sure they're reliable and space worthy."

Nat tilted her head and regarded the man with contempt on her face. "Are you calling me a liar? A captain in the Space Ranger Corps?" she asked. Again, Catherine watched the man shift his eyes from her face to Nat's and then back again. She could tell he was beginning to realize there was no easy way out of this predicament. Nat's demeanor was so intimidating, clearly holding a tone of determination, Catherine was sure the man realized he would have to make some concessions or else there would be trouble.

Holding up his hands and shaking his head in a mock appearance of resignation, he took two more steps back and cleared his throat. "I am not agreeing with any wrongdoing here," he said. "However, to show my willingness to cooperate, I will happily provide the young lady with a similar space shuttle. As luck would have it, I have another reconditioned ED-90 on the lot. Let me show it to you." Catherine could tell Nat was not thrilled with the idea of them having to utilize such an antiquated spaceship, but she also knew they did not have a lot of options.

The man led the way through the row of larger, grander starships and Catherine could not help but wish they were taking one of them instead. The tightness of Nat's jaw made

Catherine sure the woman was thinking the same. As he took them to the small spaceship, he waved his hand at the ED-90 as if it was a prime piece. "Please," he said. "Step up and take a look. Feel free to even step inside and check out the interior. I think you will be more than impressed."

Catherine heard Nat sigh. *This is not what she has in mind*, Catherine thought and slipped her hand into Nat's to give it a squeeze. "Maybe it's better than it looks," she said. Nat gave her a weak smile as she stepped past the salesman to take a closer look. Only by luck did Catherine see a flicker of movement to her left. Just in time, she realized the man was pulling a small taser from his pocket. "Nat," Catherine exclaimed. "He has a weapon."

CHAPTER 23
SAL

Sal was in the middle of a dream. A good one. Music was playing, and across the high school gym was a pretty dark-haired girl who kept sneaking glances at her. *I'm going to do it*, she thought in the dream. *I'm going to go talk to her*. With her heart racing and her mouth dry with nerves, the woman who would later be the most fearless of Space Rangers was scared half to death. Before she made it even halfway across the open space, an earsplitting screeching sound filled the air and yanked Sal from her shallow sleep. At first disoriented, Sal blinked herself awake and tried to remember where she was. The screech sounded again, and it was like nothing she ever heard before, and that was saying a lot considering all her adventures.

What in the hell was that? she thought, fully awake as the last wisps of the beautiful dream faded away. She reached for her plasma gun beside her and rolled to her knees to point it out the hole in the tree. Her best guess was some sort of bird. *But a very big bird. And let's hope I am not sitting in her nest.* Beside her, she heard Jade moving around and glanced back over her shoulder to see the woman was rubbing her eyes to get the sleep out of them.

"What was that?" she asked, and Sal shook her head.

"Your guess is as good as mine," she replied and then let her eyes drift down the woman's body. As she slowly came awake, there was a gentleness to Jade, and Sal felt the strangest desire to take her in her arms and cuddle her close.

Cuddle her close? Sal wondered. *Where is that coming from? When was the last time I wanted to cuddle anything period?* Angel's Fire did not typically make her feel romantic. On a regular night, Sal would have laid the woman back and screwed her until she screamed. Pulling off her clothes, spreading her legs, and plunging her fingers deep inside, making sure the woman knew Salishan Bransen controlled her. *But nothing happened.* Frankly, Sal was puzzled by her sudden restraint. Yet, there was something about Jade which gave her pause. *A memory of someone ...* Before she could come up with any answers, the screeching sounded again, and in an instant, all her focus snapped back to whatever was happening outside in the branches. The earsplitting sound was followed by a scrabbling noise of what could only be sharp claws on the bark. Sal knew she guessed right. The creature was some type of bird and based on proximity, it wanted to be where they were.

"I think we need to get our stuff together and vacate the premises," Sal said. "Like right now."

"Is it coming?" Jade asked while Sal heard her grabbing the duffel bag and guessed she was climbing to her feet. Appreciating the woman's response even while she asked the question, Sal stood as well. She had to duck to not hit her head in the small space, but she was ready to see what was waiting for them.

"I'll take the rifle and the bag. You take the plasma gun," Sal said as she handed over the weapon. Jade took it without comment. Sal checked to make sure her weapon was set to full power. As much as she hated the idea of killing something which was probably defending its territory, she was not going to be some bird's morning worm. Without another word, Sal stepped into the daylight. What she saw gave her pause. It was not a bird making screeching noises but instead a more reptilian looking creature. It had a long, pointed beak and black beady eyes, which now stared at Sal with curiosity. Leather-like skin covered its features, and with another screech that made Sal wince, it spread its wings, and they suddenly reminded her of a giant bat.

"My God," she heard Jade say from behind her. "It's a pterodactyl."

Sal frowned as she scanned her memory to figure out what Jade was talking about. It was not until she thought of grade school that she could place the word. *A pterodactyl?* she thought. *As in a fucking dinosaur?*

"Stay behind me," Sal said as she took a step out onto the branch, keeping herself between Jade and the creature. "Start climbing down and I'll cover you."

"But who will cover your exit?" Jade asked.

"You let me worry about that," Sal replied. "Now go." Jade did not make another comment, and Sal was glad to hear the sound of the woman climbing down. The pterodactyl eyeballed Sal who still held her rifle pointed at the thing's head. She hoped she would not have to shoot it. The beast did nothing wrong and only wanted its nest back. As if to emphasize the point, the thing opened its beak and let out another long bloodcurdling screech.

"Take it easy, mama," Sal whispered to the pterodactyl. "We'll be out of your space in two shakes." Sal watched as the beast tilted its head trying to interpret what she said. In answer, the thing moved a hair closer and this time rattled off a series of clicking noises from its throat. They were surprisingly loud, and the sound echoed through the treetops. Sal suddenly had an alarming realization. *What if she is calling more of them?* Sal thought. "How is it going?" Sal called to Jade without taking her eyes off of the prehistoric bird.

"Slow but steady," Jade replied from further away, and Sal let out a relieved breath. Then, Sal saw a flicker of movement up in the sky, and her fear was realized. There were dark specks circling in the glimpses of blue above the canopy. More pterodactyls headed their way.

"Well, as much fun as this is," Sal said to the dinosaur. "I need to go. Now do us both a favor and stay right there." With that, she slowly slung the rifle over her back and started to back away. The thing watched her but did not follow. Knowing an excellent time to go when she saw one, Sal turned in one smooth move and jumped off of the branch to cling onto the trunk of the great tree. The bark was relatively smooth under her strong hands, but like with the climb up, there were vines she could use to grip. While keeping an eye of the overhead branches in case any of the pterodactyls decided to pursue, she followed Jade down. When she saw the woman was on the ground again, Sal leaped from the tree trunk and fell the last eight feet. Landing nimbly on the balls of her feet, she twisted the rifle back around and scanned the area.

"You ready to go?" she asked, and Jade nodded, but before she could answer, there were more screeches overhead. It seemed the flock had come to roost, and they had escaped in the nick of time.

ALMOST IMMEDIATELY, Sal felt sweat trickling down the middle of her back. The humidity was not as thick as the vegetation they were forced to push through, but it was close. After an hour of struggling, Sal was relieved when they finally came to a broader path. It was trampled down enough to make a sort of a deer trail, but for something much bigger. *Elephants?* she wondered. Then, another thought came to her, and she started to scan the ground. Her eyes lit on the exact thing she hoped not to see. An animal track. A very big animal track.

"Why did we stop?" Jade asked, her breath heavy with exertion.

"I think we may have a big problem," Sal answered and meant it literally.

"What do you mean?" Jade asked as she came to stand beside her. Sal pointed a finger toward the ground to indicate the giant footprint. "I mean that," Sal answered, and Jade listened until she heard the woman suck in a breath.

"That does not look good," Jade murmured.

Sal had to agree. The footprint was easily three feet across. The thing had four toes tipped with long, very pointed claws. If she had to guess, an upright walking dinosaur made them. *Predatory dinosaur I'm guessing too,* she thought turning to look at Jade.

The woman noticed her stare. "What?" Jade asked.

Sal paused, and then she chuckled at it all because there was nothing else to do. "You picked a planet where we are at the bottom of the food chain, Jade," Sal said with a shake of her head. "All the little balls floating around in this unmapped galaxy and you managed to pick a dinosaur planet."

CHAPTER 24
NAT

She heard Catherine's warning at the same moment she saw a flash of movement. Reacting in the split second before he could activate the Taser and grab either of them, Nat randomly thought *please don't let my knee give out now* as she launched into a front kick. Her foot caught the man in the chest and sent him reeling backward. Unfortunately, he kept his feet and held the Taser in front of him as if it would be enough to protect him.

"I strongly suggest you put that thing away," Nat advised. "I am a trained Space Ranger, well-versed in hand-to-hand combat, and I will respond to your threat in the appropriate manner."

The man paused, and she watched him appraise her with a different eye. He was no longer a slimy salesman, but instead took on the appearance of a savvy streetfighter. *A gutter rat because of the nature of his business*, she thought. Buying used spaceships, particularly ones most likely stolen, meant he dealt with the most unsavory types of characters. Still, Nat felt confident. Yesterday she held her own against two other Rangers, armed with blasters. Of course, Catherine's well-timed throw gave her the last bit of advantage she needed, but Nat felt more confident than ever.

"Fuck off," the salesman spat out, and Nat shook her head.

"I'm going to count to three," she said as she took a step closer. She was pleased to see her adversary take a step back. "Drop the Taser, and I will not hurt you. One."

The man narrowed his eyes, and she knew he was calculating his odds. "I'll call the cops," he said in a voice lacking confidence. She noticed his hand was starting to shake and there was the first hint of glistening sweat on his brow.

"So call," Nat bluffed. "I'm sure they would be very interested in hearing about the sort of operation you're running here." Nat took another step closer. "Two." The man licked his lips, and Nat knew the instant before he moved he was going to lunge at her. Without thinking about it, she prepared a counterattack. As the man's arm with the Taser came toward her, she feigned going left, and when his eyes moved to follow her, she twisted into a spinning roundhouse kick. Her heel clipped the man behind the ear, and he dropped like a sack of potatoes to the pavement. It was all over in a matter of a few seconds, and Nat stood over him not quite sure what to do next.

Suddenly, Catherine was beside her. "Is he dead?" she asked, and Nat frowned. She hoped not.

"Not likely," she answered. "Now, let's see about a spaceship." In the same instant, Nat heard the sound of something beeping. Furrowing her brow, she knelt by the unconscious man. *What the hell?* she thought, patting his pockets. *Was he wearing an explosive?*

"Nat?" Catherine asked with concern in her voice. "Is that—?"

Before she could finish, Nat found the source of the sound. There was a small commlink in his coat pocket. The kind a person would activate if they were in trouble. *But who would he have wanted to contact? Certainly not the police?* she wondered. Suddenly, she did not want to be there when whoever it was showed up. "Dammit," she muttered and turned to scan the parking lot. Her eyes fell on the ED-90, and she grimaced. *There's no way I'm going to take that ship anywhere.* Looking at her other options, her eyes lit on a relatively new looking Verado 5-50, and she grinned. Seeing her look, she saw Catherine follow her gaze.

"Nat?" she asked. "Can we?"

Nat stood up from beside the still unconscious man. "Let's check his office. He must have a rack of FSD Coders to start these ships," she said.

"Are you sure?" Catherine asked. "You know they will come after us if we take something that valuable."

Nat took Catherine by the hand and led her toward the small trailer which she assumed was the salesman's office. "Catherine, they're going to be after us no matter what we do," she said, and they made their way inside the unlocked building. Considering how much of a slob the salesman appeared to be in person, his office was remarkably neat. Nat wondered if the way he dressed and kept himself was intentionally meant to disarm would-be buyers. After all, he was surprisingly fast with his defenses and even though he was no match for her, he did not back down from a fight. She would not be surprised if further investigation revealed connections with the Space Mafia. That lot of spaceships was possibly nothing more than a front to launder credits or perform other illegal activities.

All the more reason to find that coder and get the hell out of here, she thought as she made her way behind the desk trying the drawers as she went. On the third try, she found the one filled with FDR coders to start spaceships. The devices were in neat rows, but unfortunately, they were numbered but otherwise not marked. She would have to guess which might go to the Verado by the elaborateness of some of the fobs attached to the coders. *Surely, such a sporty spaceship will have a cool starter?*

Grabbing a handful of the ones which seemed the most likely, she turned to Catherine. "We have to try these one-by-one," she said.

Catherine nodded and reached out for half the pile. "I'll start at one end, and you start on the other. We can click them until something lights up."

"Perfect," Nat said as they made their way back out the door. She jogged across the parking lot and felt her knee acting up, no doubt from using it to pivot for her last kick. Gritting her teeth at the spasm shooting up her thigh, she tried to hide the pain from Catherine. *Not now,* she thought. *Please not now.*

Doing her best not to stumble, she noted the salesman was starting to stir. Nat handed the rest of the coders to Catherine. "I'm going to have to do something with him," she said with a nod at the man on the ground. "You start, and I'll see if there's a place to lock him up."

Catherine paused, looking into Nat's face, a hint of concern in her eyes. "I can see you are limping, Nat," she said. "Be careful. He looks heavy."

Nat gave her a grin. "This is nothing," she said and leaned in to give the woman a quick peck on the lips. "Now go get that Verado started." Catherine only looked half convinced but turned to hurry toward the spaceship. Nat hoped they would get lucky sooner rather than later as she remembered the device in the salesman's pocket. Help would be responding any minute now.

Paying attention to the man again, she saw he was now sitting and shaking his head to clear it. *How unfortunate,* Nat thought with a smirk as she came up behind him. *Now I have to hit him again.* Hearing her steps, the salesman spun around on his butt to locate her. His eyes widened when he saw her coming at him. "I have credits!" he offered. "Whatever you want." Nat shook her head and kept walking toward him. The man crab-walked backward, faster than she would have guessed. But not fast enough. Even with her knee spasming, she closed the distance in a flash and brought down a karate chop on the side of his neck. From her years of experience, Nat knew it would be enough to temporarily block the blood flow to his brain and cause him to pass out instantly. There would be no long-term damage, but it would give them time to escape.

As the man slid over onto his side, unconscious again, she heard the distant sounds of spaceships approaching. *Those will be his friends,* she thought needing to find Catherine who was hidden from view among the spaceships. They might need to abandon the idea of getting one and run for it. Before she could decide, she heard a promising chirp and saw the lights of the Verado flashing. A grin spread across her face. They might have to run for their lives, but at least in that ship, they would have a chance.

As she hustled in the direction of the Verado, she was pleased to see Catherine waiting for her in the doorway. She already activated the control to extend the gangway. "You're amazing," Nat said, and she approached. "I can't believe you found it so fast."

Catherine shrugged. "I've been nothing but lucky since I met you," she said. "But I think I hear someone coming."

Nat agreed. There was definitely a rumble of an oncoming starship. *More than one if I'm not mistaken*, she thought, and hoped the Verado 5-50 lived up to its reputation. "You ready to try and outrun them?" Nat asked. "We could go on foot and probably hide."

In answer, Catherine gave her a wink. "I'm ready to see you fly this thing, Captain," she said, and Nat liked the sound of that. She liked it very much indeed.

CHAPTER 25
JADE

For Jade, it did not take much convincing on Sal's part to get her to turn around and find a different path. The dinosaur tracks in the mud upset her badly. Much more than she was willing to let on. Although as a Space Ranger she went on missions which led to planets on the outskirts of the known galaxies, she always traveled as a part of a large squad. The teams consisted of Rangers experienced in different terrains. Jade was never dispatched to a location so remote as this one however and certainly never with only one other person as support. *Although Sal is more like half a dozen other people*, she thought. Still, it was unsettling, and she quickened her pace to stay close to the other woman.

As she followed Sal, who pushed through the vegetation back the way they came, Jade could not help but wonder what might become of them with only the resources they carried. It was not like they could use the commlink to call for help. They were most likely out of range of any ships or inhabited planets. Then there was the fact they were fugitives. *I am a fugitive*, she repeated in her mind. The entire situation completely unsettled her. *How could this all have happened?* Being forced to flee was not in her master plan. She was not supposed to be at Sal's mercy. Yet as another large branch threatened to slap her in the face, Jade moved up even closer to the tall, broad-shouldered woman. Salishan Bransen was her lifeline, and Jade knew it.

Keeping up her pace, having no idea where they were going, Jade let her thoughts wander back to the original mission. They were yet to truly debrief what happened back at the compound. So far, she was left with Sal's flippant explanation of what she saw when she found the president. The ex-Space Ranger was convinced the events were all part of a setup, yet Jade could not believe it in her heart. Doing so would mean admitting the Space Rangers turned their back on her. There was more to the story, she knew it. *But finding answers will be next to impossible while we are on this godforsaken planet*, she thought. *Until I can ask some questions, there will be no way to unravel this mystery*. She puffed out a frustrated breath but kept walking.

Ducking to go under a thick brown and green vine, Jade nearly ran into the back of Sal who suddenly stopped. "Wha—?" she started to say when Sal spun on her quickly covering Jade's mouth with her hand. The woman's dark eyes were even more severe than usual, and Jade could tell by her face whatever was in front of them was not good. Slowly, she tilted her head to see around Sal's shoulder. Her stomach clenched with fear. In the opening among the giant trees, a reptilian-like dinosaur the size of a bus was eating. *An incredibly scary looking dinosaur*. The thing's muzzle of sharp teeth tore into the side of a second large creature. The beast did not yet notice them, hence the reason Sal preferred for them to keep silent and immobile.

What's next? she thought hoping Sal could read her mind. Suddenly, it did not matter as Jade watched the hungry dinosaur's yellow eyes turn in their direction. In their depths, Jade saw its recognition of prey, and she knew they were in serious trouble. When the beast lifted its head, and she saw blood dripping from its jaw, Jade's heart thundered in her chest. Suddenly, Sal's hand over her mouth was smothering. Starting to choke, she could not catch her breath. Every instinct in her body was to run, and as if sensing those feelings, Sal moved her face closer until they were eye to eye. The woman mouthed the words "Back up slowly," and Jade gave a subtle nod of her head. As she started taking one step back, she saw a flicker of something that could almost be described as fear pass over Sal's face. The woman's eyes stared past Jade's shoulder and back down the gap they came through into the clearing. Whatever concerned Jade paled by comparison to the sight Sal was seeing over her shoulder. *If Sal is afraid,* she thought. *I really don't want to know.*

Slowly, Sal straightened. She let the duffle bag fall from her shoulder while slipping the laser rifle from her back and brought it around in one quick motion. Not sure what was happening, Jade twisted to look behind her and realized she was right. She did not want to know what thing scared Sal. An almost identical dinosaur, only perhaps even bigger to the eater in the clearing was walking toward them. As it neared, she felt a slight trembling of the earth, barely perceptible over the pounding of her heart. "Oh my God," she whispered. "We're trapped." Two giant predators were closing in on them with nowhere to run.

"Yes, it's a problem," Sal growled. "But this isn't over yet." The woman grabbed Jade's shoulder and started to pull her back into the clearing where that first dinosaur was standing up from his supper. She was not sure what Sal's plan was, but she went along anyway because she knew if anyone could get them out of this it would be the ex-Space Ranger. With the rifle still trained on the oncoming dinosaur, she watched Sal glance back at the carcass on the ground. "Let's hope they ignore us and fight over that."

With Sal still aiming the rifle but not taking a shot, Jade wondered if it was because the blast from the gun might only do subliminal damage to the thick scales of the reptilian creatures. *It would most likely piss them off*, she thought. Suddenly, the oncoming dinosaur stopped at the edge of the clearing and let out a roar so ferocious, Jade stumbled as she backed up beside Sal. She never heard anything more terrifying, and tears sprang to her eyes. Before any fell, a hysterical laugh bubbled up inside her. They were probably going to die a horrible death, yet she laughed as she thought of the crazy last forty-eight hours. It seemed she was set up for an assassination, went on the run, jumped through a wormhole, and ended up on a dinosaur planet caught between two gigantic predators. It seemed impossible, yet here she was, about to die. The only thing that could make the situation even more unbelievable was if they were suddenly rescued. At that moment, she saw a flicker of movement to her left and turned expecting to see yet another monster, but instead found herself staring into the eyes of what appeared to be a little boy.

Jade squeezed her eyes shut. When she reopened them, she still saw the face looking out at her from between the leaves. As she watched she noticed the boy's skin tone changed as the leaves swayed in the wind. *He's a chameleon,* she thought and realized it was perfect camouflage when having to hide from predators like the two bearing down on them. Only the whites of the boy's eyes gave him away, and she knew if he closed them and stepped back, he would be invisible to her. Not taking her eyes from him, Jade flapped her hand until she hit Sal's arm. She didn't dare look away from the boy's face in case he disappeared. "Sal," she said. When it was no answer, she slapped harder. "Sal," she repeated with more emphasis.

"I'm a wee bit busy here," Sal hissed.

Jade kept slapping. "Look at this, Sal," Jade insisted, and she felt the woman come closer.

"You've got to be kidding," Jade heard Sal say. "Kid, can you get us out of here?" Jade saw the boy start to retreat. Not hesitating, Jade grabbed the duffle bag at her feet and plunged into the brush after him. She felt Sal's hand on her lower back pushing her along. There was another roar behind them, and Jade hoped the two predators were going at each other, taking no interest in the lowly humans slipping away. Before they went ten feet, Jade realized they were on a narrow path, imperceptible from the original clearing. Not far ahead was the boy. He wore what looked like it might be leather, but it was hard to tell as his skin continued to change color as he moved from one plant to the next. Every few feet, he would pause his scampering to look back and make sure they were still following. Jade had no idea where they were headed, but at that point, she could not care less as long as they were moving away from the fighting dinosaurs behind them.

CHAPTER 26
CATHERINE

Sitting in the jumpseat behind Nat, Catherine watched over her shoulder as they broke through the Untas atmosphere and shot into space. Letting out the breath she did not realize she held, Catherine let herself relax a little. Disbelief they got away filled her. When she first heard the roar of oncoming spaceships back at the lot, Catherine saw no way they could escape. Their pursuers were too close. Even as Nat engaged the thrusters and lifted them off the asphalt, Catherine expected blasts to start coming in their direction. She was not naive enough to think the men the slimy salesman worked for would be satisfied with asking questions. Everything had a shoot first feel to it. Before she asked Nat what her plan was, the woman barked out a laugh. *What could be funny at this moment?* Catherine wondered.

"What?" she asked, and Nat glanced over her shoulder at her with a wide grin on her face.

"I do believe this used to be a smuggler's ship," she replied.

A smuggler's ship? Catherine thought. *Why would that matter?* As she was about to ask, Nat pointed to a black device hidden partially under the front console of the cockpit.

"I don't know what that is," Catherine said as Nat began to work the thing's instrument panel, which suddenly glowed to life.

"It's a cloaking device," she replied, punching in digits on the screen's display.

Catherine raised her eyebrows. "As in, it will make us invisible?" Catherine asked, suddenly filled with hope they were not going to be shot out of the sky at any minute.

"Exactly that," Nat answered. "I won't get into all the details of how the transparency feature works. But it can bounce back light, making us appear as nothing more than a shimmer."

"Like a trick of the eye," Catherine added, now understanding and watching as Nat tapped one last button. As she did it, Catherine felt the slightest vibration pass through the ship. Green lights showed on the device and Nat clapped her hands.

"I do believe that will do the trick," she said, reversing the thrusters to take the ship down to a much slower rate. "We have to be careful no one runs into us by accident."

Catherine nodded at the logic. Being invisible could have unfortunate side effects. Still, she felt relieved and put her hand on Nat's shoulder. The woman turned her head and kissed the back of Catherine's hand, and although it was tender, Catherine felt the excitement running through her lover. Catherine knew the months as a trainer at the academy were harder on Nat than she ever admitted. But now there was this new adventure, and she saw how it was making the woman so much more alive. It made Catherine's heart happy to see, even in the middle of all the danger.

"Well, look at this," Nat said, now leaning to the right and tapping another spot on the dash. "I think I'm in love." She laughed, and Catherine smiled at the sound of it. The joy in her voice had been missing, and she did not realize until just then for how long.

Putting on a sultry smile, Catherine tilted her head. "Should I be jealous?" she asked, and Nat returned the smile with a sexy one of her own as she shook her head.

"No, never," she replied. "But I am going to be very fond of this spaceship, I can tell. The smugglers went for the full meal deal when they ordered up this one. Cloaking device and then look at this." Nat pointed, and Catherine moved forward to see another screen with even more digital sliders and switches.

"What will that do?" she asked, and Nat's grin grew even broader.

"These are an extra set of boosters," she explained. "This baby is built for speed. I think we're going to have some fun."

As if to prove it, Nat engaged the extra power, checked the radar for any nearby craft, and then rocketed them off the planet. Within moments, they were moving through the inky blackness of space, leaving Untas and any pursuers in their wake.

"Pull up the orbital positioning system, if you don't mind," Nat said as she put the ship on cruise control. "And let's pop in this planet coordinate. I want to see where our old friend Sal has got herself off to."

Liking the sound of that, Catherine unhooked her seatbelt and moved closer to Nat so she could activate the system. As the 3-D map lit up, she placed her fingers on the keypad, ready to enter the information Nat would relay to her. Nat pulled a piece of paper from her pocket with the number written on it.

To keep from being tracked, she transcribed it back at the hotel before destroying her commlink.

"173482-B11," Nat read, and Catherine typed it in. As they watched, the display zoomed across the 8th Galaxy until it came to a less defined area. Catherine guessed the location was relatively unexplored based on the lack of clarity of the different planets in that zone. It was also a significant distance if she understood the metrics ticking off above the hologram.

Why would she be clear out there? Catherine wondered. *Has she been hiding there all along?* She always imagined Sal was in the middle of some large city, hiding in plain sight and living an exciting, albeit underground, life.

"Interesting," Nat said. "There must be a wormhole between here and there. It's too far to fly, even using hyperspace. Means she's on the run though."

Catherine furrowed her brow. "Why?" she asked.

Nat looked at her with a raised eyebrow. "Does the Sal you know look like the person who would chill out on some remote, unexplored rock under normal circumstances?" she asked.

Catherine shook her head. "No," she said. "But it doesn't mean she did it."

With a sigh, Nat nodded. "I know. It has me thinking otherwise. If she did the crime, there would have been a big payout of credits I imagine. Sal's not going to be able to spend them in the middle of nowhere." Then, Nat paused, and Catherine watched her consider the image of the planet again. "Unless there is another space pirate stronghold out here which no one knows about. After all, it is Sal."

Catherine considered the possibility, but the idea did not feel right. Not space pirates. "You don't think she's gone back with them though?" Catherine asked as a sense of unease tightened her stomach. *Surely Sal would not have resorted to that,* she hoped.

"No," Nat said after a pause. "I don't think that. My gut tells me different. I think if I had to guess, I think she was somehow cooperating with the Space Ranger's and put in a position to be set up."

Catherine nodded. She considered that a possibility too. A setup certainly made some things fall into place. "Do you think so?" she asked.

"Yes," Nat said relaxing in the captain's chair as the ship moved on autopilot at lightspeed through space. "I've given this some thought. If it was me, what would put me in the position Sal is in? It has to be a setup."

Catherine's heart rejoiced to hear Nat considering Sal a peer. She always knew they were cut from the same cloth, but Nat never wanted to admit it. *Until now,* she thought. "And what was your conclusion?" Catherine asked. "You think Sal was set up, but ...?"

"That is the question," Nat said running her hand over her face. "Until we find Sal, you probably won't have an answer." Reaching out, she pulled Catherine onto her lap and looked hard into her face. Her eyes were serious. "But I will admit, in my heart, I do not believe Salishan Bransen assassinated the president. Although there might not be honor left in her on the surface, I believe she still carries it at her core. She would never be a hero without it."

Catherine nodded. She could not agree more. "Well, then let's find her," she said suddenly having a mischievous idea. "How long do you think it will take to get to where Sal is?"

Nat turned back to the orbital positioning system and quickly typed in information to run the calculation. "Well, there are three wormhole combinations between here and the edge of the known galaxy," Nat said. "If the coordinate she left us is accurate, we know the planet she's on." She pointed at a spot on the glowing virtual map. "If we go to this wormhole, we can slip through using hyperspace. But it will probably take us the rest of the afternoon at least to get there."

Catherine smiled. That was precisely what she was hoping Nat would say. Running her eyes over the woman's handsome face, she felt a tingle flutter through her. "So, you're saying we have a little spare time?" Catherine asked, her voice suddenly huskier. She loved the hungry look that leaped int her lover's eyes.

"I might be saying that," Nat replied in a soft voice. "Did you have something you needed to do?"

Catherine bit her bottom lip. "I was thinking about when we first met," she said. "Do you remember?"

Catherine watched Nat take a deep breath as if trying to figure out what Catherine was up to. "Of course, I remember," she answered. "You crashed on Taswa, and I carried you back to my ship to revive you."

Catherine nodded. "Exactly," she agreed moving in closer to look into Nat's blue eyes. "And then what happened?" She watched Nat actually blush, and the sweetness of it tickled Catherine, to see her powerful Space Ranger suddenly a bit timid.

"I took off your clothes," Nat replied. "And snuggled against you to help bring up your body temperature."

Catherine slipped even closer and cupped Nat's face. She leaned in until their lips almost touched. "And when I woke up," Catherine whispered. "I was in the arms of the most wonderful woman in the world. Who I loved from that first second, even though I did not yet know it. My hero." She heard Nat suddenly suck in a breath and knew all the excitement shivering through Catherine, her lover felt as well.

"Catherine," Nat breathed, wanting thick in her voice.

"I want to reenact that moment," Catherine said. "Only a little bit differently this time. Come with me into the back and take off my clothes. And make me warm again."

CHAPTER 27
SAL

They followed the boy in and around the giant ferns and trees traveling away from the clearing where the two dinosaurs were growling and hissing. Sal hoped the noise meant they were preparing to fight over the carcass. *And are not coming after us*, she thought as she moved nimbly down the narrow, almost invisible path. She knew the only reason they were able to find their way was because they were following the kid. Without him, they would have never found it and by now, would have been lunch.

As they rounded a bend in the path, Sal checked their backtrail and was relieved to see it was clear. She started to let herself relax a little. Being out of the dinosaur's sight meant they most likely would not follow. Picking up her pace to close the gap behind Jade, Sal suddenly heard crashing behind her. *Well, so much for not following*, she thought and started to run. She watched as the boy stopped and turned back, hearing the noise. His eyes widened, and his color changes sped up. *Because he knows one of them is coming*, she thought, and she gripped the laser rifle tighter preparing to turn and fight if necessary. It would probably be fruitless, but she would never give up without taking a stand. As if reading her mind and not wanting her to stop yet, the boy frantically waved her forward. The ground shook, but Sal did not look and instead continued to run along the path. Her shoulders tightened, and the skin on her neck crawled as she imagined that at any second, the gaping mouth of one of the giants was going to come down on her. Sal was not one to typically feel fear but being a dino snack did unnerve her a little.

Then, she was beside Jade and the waiting boy. "Why the hell have we stopped?" she hissed and felt a small hand on her arm. Looking, she saw a second face. This one looked feminine but otherwise was the same. She was apparently another guide arriving from what seemed like nowhere. In that instant, Sal realized these were not children but only small adults of an alien race she did not recognize. *Well, let's hope they know how to get us out of here*, she thought, and as if in answer, the second alien took her hand. With one last glance back in the direction of the now shaking foliage, she led Sal off the path. They plunged into the thick growth and battled for a few feet. The terrain was so dense, Sal needed to crouch almost to her hands and knees to keep moving. Her height put her at a severe disadvantage as the shorter female swiftly ducked under the leaves of the thick bushes and vines.

Seeing a particularly low overhang coming, Sal knew she was going to have to make a choice. Crawl on her belly and leave herself vulnerable to attack or stand and fight. Sal did not do well with vulnerable. Luckily, she noticed the little woman stopped and was waiting at the edge of the obstacle. Approaching, Sal noticed a hole in the ground. The alien waved for Sal to follow a moment before she dropped into the darkness. Not pausing, but not thrilled with the idea of disappearing into God knew where, Sal slung the rifle across her back, took a deep breath and stepped into the opening to follow.

At first, everything was pitch black, and the way down to the hole was steep. Sal braced herself against the cold stone of the sides to keep from rolling forward. Rifle bouncing against the back of her head, she hoped the grade of the tunnel would not get any worse or she would be doing a somersault. As she felt gravity starting to win the battle, she saw a glimmer of light ahead a moment before landing in a large cavern. The view was so stunning, Sal paused to take it in. As Jade joined her at the base of the hole, she heard the woman gasp. "It's incredible."

The space was filled with glowing purple crystals, each of them easily as long as Sal was tall. They hung from the ceiling and pushed up from the floor, and it was enough to take even her breath away. They glowed from within and gave the cavern a violet light, but it was not unpleasant. Looking around, Sal could tell the place was inhabited often. Perhaps not as a regular place to live but as a refuge to hide. As the first alien, the male Sal assumed, slipped past them and went to join his friend in the center of the room, Sal followed. *At least the ceiling is high enough, I don't have to duck,* she thought weaving around stalagmites. No doubt hearing her footsteps, the alien couple waited with what she took to be smiles. Without lips per se and stubby yellow teeth, it was hard to say for sure. "Don't suppose you speak Galaxian?" Sal asked. It was the universal language of the 8th Galaxy, and she knew if there was any chance of communicating, Galaxian was their best shot.

The little man blinked and looked puzzled. Glancing at his partner, Sal saw he was confirming her lack of understanding, too. Sal tried again in a different language. Still nothing. She tried another half dozen variations of the numerous alien styles she knew from years of traveling the galaxy. None of them worked.

"Ideas?" she asked Jade who stood beside her. The woman pursed her lips, quiet for a moment, and then spoke in yet a different dialect. In response, the female chirped a few lines of her own, and the language was truly different than any Sal ever heard. "Nice. What did she say?"

Jade shook her head. "No idea," she responded, and Sal frowned.

"Well, what did you say to them?" she asked

Jade sighed. "Where's the library?" she answered. "It's the only sentence I remember from my high school Spenlian language class."

Sal rolled her eyes. "Perfect," she said. "Well, unfortunately, we don't have a digital translator, so we are going to have to make do." She plastered on the biggest smile she could muster motioning toward herself. "I'm Sal," she said feeling a bit like an idiot but rolling with it. She pointed and said, "This is Jade." The two aliens only stared. *Great,* Sal thought. *This planet gets better and better.* Letting out a calming breath, she motioned toward the closest purple boulder. "Mind if I have a seat?" she asked the couple. When they did not respond with anything more than a few blinks, Sal took the initiative and sat. This set off a flurry of chirping, but Sal sensed no hostility. *Still, maybe sitting on this crystal is a bad move.* For all she knew, the damn things were radioactive. She turned to the little aliens and held out her hands, palms up. "So, what now?" Her pantomime seemed to do it, and the female looking of the alien pair waved for Sal to follow.

As all four moved deeper into the cavern, Sal was pleased to see a more lived-in looking area. There were boulders to sit on which were not glowing, and the cold ashes of a firepit. Glancing up, Sal noted a fissure in the ceiling where the smoke would escape. *That works*, she thought, but not planning to stay long enough to need a fire. Reaching the center of the space, both aliens started chirping and waving for Sal and Jade to take a seat.

"Please tell me you have some sort of plan," Jade whispered from close behind her. Sal glanced over, thankful to see the woman still had the duffel bag. Inside there were at least some packets of water they could drink. She wasn't quite ready to trust anything on the planet yet.

"Pull up a rock," she answered. "Take a load off until the coast is clear. I don't think these two mean us any harm."

Jade nodded. "I agree," she said and moved to sit on one that looked more like a log. The little male followed her, and when she sat, he pointed at the duffle bag. She looked up to catch Sal's eye, but sharing the contents with these two seemed only fair. She shrugged.

"Show them what we got," she said, and Jade unzipped the duffel bag. Unsurprisingly, he was very curious about the contents. The female joined him, and they took the chirping up a notch with each item Jade pulled out to show them. Sal wondered how advanced these people were and looking over their bodies she noted the clothing was rudimentary. He was wearing a pair of shorts of a material she did not recognize, while the female wore a tunic of the same mystery cloth. *A tanned hide from some other kind of dinosaur?* she wondered. One of those giant hides could go a long way. Still, the wardrobe was not much, and it made her think more of a tribal existence than anything advanced. *Just our luck.* Sal hoped to find people who had the means of flying off the planet or even possibly sending another communication, but clearly, these were not them.

CHAPTER 28
JADE

She and Sal sat in the cavern eating power bars. They offered some to what Jade now realized were adult aliens and not children, but both declined. After sniffing the food and examining the wrapper, each of them handed it back with what Jade took as a smile of thanks, but no thanks. She did not hold it against them considering the thick, dehydrated protein bar had the flavor of a piece of cardboard and sat in her stomach much the same way cardboard would. As she finished, she let her eyes wander the room and noticed on the far wall, across the open floor of the cavern, was what looked like etchings. Curious, she stood and walked to them.

"Everything okay?" Sal asked.

Jade nodded and let her gaze fall on the artwork scratched there. She knew petroglyphs in caves found on many planets of the galaxy represented the history of the different races. Based on what she could tell from these drawings, they were the same. There were stick figures of what she assumed were the same race as the two aliens who helped them. There was a group fighting what could only be taken as the same type of monster which nearly ate her and Sal. The picture denoted a battle where the aliens poked at the thing with spears. She could not help but be disappointed they did not have more sophisticated technology.

Running her eyes along the sequence of events she wondered if she was going back in time through the years of their existence. Stepping to her left, she kept going until she came across something that made her catch her breath. There was a larger sketch which was elaborate and carved with a sharper tool than the others. The image was of a massive spaceship, and it appeared to have crashed into the jungle. "Sal," Jade said with excitement. "You should come take a look at this."

She heard Sal come up behind her and waited for the woman's reaction. "You have to be kidding me," Sal said, but Jade heard a hint of excitement in her voice as well. *Could it be possible that somewhere in the jungle was an old spaceship?* Jade thought. This one was large and no doubt a transport of some kind as opposed to something smaller like a fighter. It did not take a stretch of the imagination to think the two aliens and their people came originally from that starship. "We need to check this out," Jade said and out of the corner of her eye she saw Sal turn to look back at their hosts. Jade followed her gaze to see the two little aliens still standing in the center of the room watching them. It was impossible to read their features as they were so different than her own, but if she had to guess the aliens were puzzled by their interest in the picture. Sal walked over and dropped to one knee. She pointed at the spaceship etched into the wall.

"Take us to this?" Sal asked even though Jade knew it was probably futile. The male and female both shrugged their shoulders. Sal pointed again and then mimicked walking with her fingers. This time a hint of understanding appeared in the male alien's eyes, and he started a long bout of chirping to his friend. Jade realized he grasped what Sal wanted. *Oh, thank God*, she thought. For the moment, maybe her luck was changing.

FOLLOWING A PATH, WHICH was only slightly wider than the one they escaped on, Jade did her best to keep up with the pair of aliens in front of her. As soon as the male realized where they wanted to go, and he let the female know, they moved quickly. She and Sal hurried to gather up their gear before losing the pair in the cavern. Luckily, they did not take the steep tunnel back up the way they came and instead went through a series of smaller and smaller caverns until they emerged at the side of the hill. It was a little unnerving, because Jade had no idea where they were in relation to the lake. She could only hope Sal's sense of direction was better.

When they emerged, she glanced around to try and locate the high peak she and Sal initially headed toward, but the canopy overhead was too thick. It almost completely blocked out the sun, and giant ferns covered the ground. Walking took concentration because if someone moved even a few feet to the left or the right of the narrow trail, a person could get lost. She realized the maze could only be navigated by experienced inhabitants of the jungle. If she ever became turned around it would be likely she would never find her way back. *Let's hope it doesn't ever come to that*, she thought.

Turning past another giant tree, Jade glanced over her shoulder to see Sal was only a few paces behind. Jade noticed the woman was continually checking in all directions. She furrowed her brow. If she did not know better, she would think Sal was worried about a trap. *Should I be worried?* Jade wondered. *Are these two aliens not what they appear?* To her thinking, they were nothing but little aliens on a planet at the edge of the 8th Galaxy who had not met humans before. After all, they saved them from being eaten by the dinosaurs and for that she was grateful. *Sal's just being Sal.*

Finally, after what felt like more than a half dozen kilometers, they emerged into an open field. The grass was almost to her waist making it a challenge to see the two guides as the grass reached their chins. The female, in front, slowed her pace considerably, no doubt realizing it was harder to see her in the tall grass. They only hiked a minute more when suddenly Jade heard Sal growl. Spinning to look, she saw Sal bring the rifle up in a defensive posture. Alarmed, Jade scanned all around them but saw nothing but grass. "What is it?" Jade asked. Sal continued to study the landscape for more movement.

"There are others out here in the grass with us," Sal answered without looking at her. "I can hear them even if I can't see them."

Jade looked around again and tried hard to listen for any unusual sounds. There was nothing but a slight breeze pushing the grass. She started to shake her head, when she suddenly heard something, too. It was almost imperceptible, and she was amazed for a moment how sharp Sal's senses were when it came to danger. She made a mental note not to forget it.

Pulling the plasma gun from her waistband, Jade crouched so only her head poked above the top of the grass and waited for whatever was about to come after them. Her heart thudded in her chest as she considering what they encountered so far on this planet. Absolutely anything could be out there. *A giant snake?* she wondered and shivered at the thought. *Or maybe another type of dinosaur? Something short but lethal?* Glancing at Sal, she saw the woman ducking down until she was nearly hidden in the grass, rifle at the ready. Jade took some comfort from Sal's vigilance. She remembered Sal's shooting on the rooftop when the Fergs attacked her and knew her aim was true. If anything was stupid enough to pop its head up out of the grass, Sal would no doubt blow it off.

Then, Jade heard a louder noise to her left and looked back up the trail. She brought her weapon around only to realize it was the same little alien man who guided them before. He held his hands up in the universal sign of surrender, and Jade lowered the plasma gun to point toward the ground. She did not put it away, but she thought it was only fair to not keep it in his face. "What's happening?" she asked though knew it was futile. Only this time he nodded as if he understood and he stepped aside to reveal an even smaller alien. The alien stepped past the man, and Jade took in her features. Her skin was more wrinkled and weathered and if she had to guess, Jade would say the alien was significantly older than the other two. Her clothing was more ceremonial, and Jade raised her eyebrows when she realized around the alien's neck hung what she at first thought was a medallion but was in fact from a piece of machinery. *Could that be from the spaceship in the petroglyphs? Does it symbolize she is some tribal leader?*

The woman slowly moved closer. "That's far enough," Sal ordered, and Jade wondered what she saw in this petite creature which made her still wary. *Perhaps because there is still rustling in the grass?*

"I mean you no harm," the older alien replied, and Jade gasped. The accent was heavy, but it was the universal language of the 8th Galaxy. Then, she appeared to smile, and although it did not look human, it gave Jade some reassurance they were not about to be attacked. The rustle from the grass grew louder, and she turned to look in time to see Sal spin around. She pointed the rifle at six other aliens who appeared on the trail behind them. They were not armed with anything obvious aside from knives in belts at their waist, but it was still a little unnerving to be outnumbered and trapped between the two parties.

"Don't shoot them," Jade murmured. "I don't like how this feels, but I don't think we're in jeopardy either. Let's see what they want."

At first, she thought Sal would disregard her advice and blast the aliens, but then the woman slowly lowered the rifle. "I agree," she said with a nod. "Plus, I need to see that spaceship. But it doesn't mean I like this setup."

Jade agreed with Sal. She didn't like it either, but the only hope of getting off of this planet was to find some technology. Hopefully, the old spaceship was it.

CHAPTER 29
SAL

When she saw the wreck of the behemoth starship in the distance, Sal's heart sank a little. She recognized it only from pictures, as it was a relic and well over a century old. *A TDC-0424 Esla galaxy cruiser*, Sal thought. A top of the line long range colonization ship back in the day, which helped settle vast parts of the 8th Galaxy. Time and improvements in space travel rendered them obsolete, but Sal could appreciate the magnificence of the old vessel before her. *But can there possibly be any remnants of the original power source left alive on it?* It seemed impossible, but Sal would not give up hope. Usually, her luck ran hot, and she hoped, in this case, it would hold true, although, as of late, things were not necessarily going her way. *In fact,* she thought. *My luck has been horrible ever since I met Jade Hamilton.* It was something she would need to analyze, but not now. "Wow," she heard Jade say in front of her as the old alien woman led them closer and into a large clearing among a grove of giant trees.

"Hell, yeah, wow," Sal answered. "I never expected to ever lay eyes on one of these, but we might as well be in a museum."

Jade nodded. "We won't be leaving here on that," she said.

Sal agreed. "Let's hope there is still some tiny bit of sizzle left in those batteries," Sal answered.

"And then what?" Jade asked, and Sal realized she had yet to explain to the woman the encrypted message she sent to Nat. *Because I didn't trust her then*, Sal thought. *Is that still the case? Was she part of my setup or only a victim too?* As a rule, Sal never trusted anyone initially. In her experience, most people wanted something or were playing an angle. She did not hold it against anyone. Sal had agendas of her own, but considering Jade was nearly shot down alongside her, Sal believed the woman was as much a fugitive as she was. The Space Rangers turned their back on them both.

Making up her mind, Sal took Jade's arm to stop her progress and looked her hard in the eyes. "Let's say that last ditch message I sent might be my ace in the hole," Sal said. "We might have a way off of here yet." Jade opened her mouth to comment, but before she could, the old alien woman stopped and turned to them.

"Welcome," she said, and Sal looked around recognizing they had reached something of a village. Many of the huts were well camouflaged in the jungle along the perimeter of where the ship partially embedded in the dirt long ago. As she watched, the alien opened her arms wide in further greeting, and Sal saw the jungle come alive with movement. Before she could even raise her rifle, dozens upon dozens of other aliens who looked like the others stepped forward. They were all small but presented in many sizes, and Sal realized she was looking at generations. Everything from weathered and old to babies in arms. One thing was for sure, among them Sal felt like a giant. They were apparently as awestruck by her height and lighter skin as she was at their appearance as all stared and slowly, some of the braver aliens moved forward.

Taking it all in, Sal realized the six males who were at the rear of their line hiking in were taking a defensive posture. She could already guess what was coming next and she wanted no part of it. When one of the tallest of the alien males came to her with his hand outstretched, Sal knew he was going to ask her to hand over her weapons. "Screw that," Sal muttered and gripped the rifle tighter. Jade stepped closer and held her plasma gun in her hand as well. Neither of them was pointing the weapons at anyone in particular, but it was clear they were at a bit of a standoff. The last thing Sal wanted was to start blasting into these aliens. Particularly when there were children and babies among them, but she was not about to become a captive either. She grit her teeth. There was a decision to make, and she did not like her options.

Suddenly, the old woman, who was clearly a leader of the tribe, snapped some chirps at the male who was looking at Sal's rifle. She had no idea what the alien said, but if she was going to guess, it was telling everyone to back off.

"Please excuse my grandson," the alien explained. "We are not used to new faces. He is ... what is the word? Paranoid?"

Sal let out the breath she did not realize she was holding and nodded. "Paranoid is a good word for it," she answered. "Can you explain I like to keep my weapons close?"

The alien chirped something at her grandson, who chirped back and shot Sal an angry look, but then he backed away. "You may keep your weapon," the old woman said. "But it makes him and some of the others very upset."

Sal frowned. She knew she needed this tribe's help if she was going to escape from the planet. *Hell, I need them to survive on this planet,* she thought and decided at that moment she would trust the old woman. Quite possibly with her life. She must take the risk; it was as simple as that. She needed access to the crashed starship to see what was available to set up a beacon to signal Nat. Squaring her shoulders and hoping she was not making a hell of a mistake, Sal pointed the rifle down and held it out for the grandson.

"Sal, what are you doing?" Jade asked with a hint of alarm in her voice.

"I'm trusting them," Sal responded and looked at the alien leader. "I accept your welcome. We are honored to be your guests." The grandson stepped forward and with a nod of appreciation took the rifle. Next, he stepped over to Jade. Sal watched him tilt his head again, using body language to ask the question of what Jade was going to do. She saw the woman glance in her direction and Sal nodded, which was enough for Jade to relinquish the weapon. It left Sal with only her knife, which she was not going to give up. Thankfully, the grandson made no issue of it, and Sal realized all the males, and many of the females wore knives too. She could appreciate that, as she survived many a battle with only her blade, and if it came to it, she would survive with it in her hand again.

Once the weapons were whisked away, the old alien woman turned back to Sal and Jade. "Thank you for your trust," she said. "Now, what can we do for you? I imagine you did not expect to be here on Audarg with us."

Sal nodded grateful the leader was wise enough to recognize the situation. "No," Sal agreed. "We did not, or at least not without our ship. We crashed."

The old alien woman laughed softly. "Oh, I know about crashes," she said with a glance back at the colossal wreck of a spaceship.

Sal followed her look and understood. This tribe was descendants of whatever race was on the transport. *And they were never rescued?* Sal wondered, starting to lose hope there was a transmitter they could activate. *If they could not call for help then ... Still, there may be enough to set up a radio beacon.* Sal needed a way to signal Nat when she came. *Assuming she got the message and decided to come after me.* Sal realized she was putting a lot of stock in Nat. Something in her gut told her Catwoman had read the message and was underway. Sal could never put words to the feeling of connection between them, but in her core, she was confident the Space Ranger would not let her down.

Then, Sal thought of Catherine. She wondered if Catherine heard the news Sal was accused of assassinating the president of the 8th Galaxy. *And if she did, what does she think?* she wondered. *Will she believe it?* Somehow, she was sure the woman would not. It gave Sal confidence, that if Catherine knew about the distress call, she would implore Nat to follow it. *Perhaps come with her on the rescue?* The idea of seeing Catherine again made a tightness form in Sal's chest. Although she knew Catherine loved only Nat, there was something about her Sal could not get out of her head. A special feeling toward her she had not felt for a very long time. *Not since ...* Sal started to think, but then shut it down. She did not want to think about her past right now. Thinking about the things she could not change was pointless, and she knew it. Instead, she looked the old woman in her eyes. "I'd like a tour of your spaceship," she said.

The old woman smiled before nodding. "Of course," she said and turned to lead them toward the starship. "Follow me."

CHAPTER 30
NAT

As they entered the uncharted planet's atmosphere, Nat could not think of a time in the last six months she felt better than right now. The idea of exploring new territory coming on the heels of an incredible late afternoon lovemaking with Catherine put her in the highest spirits. She admitted, she thought her life of adventure was over, and then fate put her on an entirely different path in the blink of an eye. The trick though would be finding Sal. As if reading her mind, Catherine came into the cockpit and put a hand on Nat's shoulder. "How in the universe are we going to find her?" the younger woman asked. "Is this a very big planet?"

Nat answered by pulling up the holographic display of the planet. She reflected on the sphere floating in space and noted the metrics rattling up the side of the projection. The planet was quite large and comparable to some others Nat was familiar with. "About the size of Prospo," she answered, knowing Catherine would be able to use that as a good point of reference. She grew up there, and Nat held fond memories of the place as it was where she first got to know Catherine. Someday they could return to enjoy another time there like the last.

Catherine frowned. "In that case, it will make our search especially hard, right?" she asked.

Nat nodded. "I'm afraid so," she answered. "Unless Sal comes up with some way to signal us, we might have a problem." She pointed to a place on the planet where they were crossing and zoomed in hoping to pick up heat signatures that might reflect humans. There were several large blips, but she knew they could not be Sal because they were so big. *Really big*, Nat thought as she pondered what the blips could be. *What kind of planet is this?* There was only one good way to find out. "Ready to take a peek?"

Glancing over her shoulder, she saw the young woman slip into the jumpseat and attach her seatbelt. An excited glimmer shone in her wide eyes, and she nodded. "I can't wait," she said, and Nat smiled. *I so love her*, she thought and in response dipped the spaceship toward the surface.

As they soared over the canopy of dense trees, Nat frowned. Even with radar, she was having trouble seeing anything useful. "Hmmm, I don't see much," Nat said when suddenly something substantial flew up in front of the ship. With split-second reflexes, Nat cut left. It was a near miss and she heard Catherine gasp.

"My God, what was that?" she asked.

Nat shook her head, not ready to believe her eyes. "Honestly, I think it was something we learned in grade school," she answered.

"I think I have to agree with you. Pterodactyl?" Catherine responded.

"Incredible, but yes," Nat said.

"What kind of planet is this?" Catherine asked. Nat shook her head. She could not be entirely sure yet, but if she was going to guess, they were on a dinosaur planet. She never experienced one in all her travels with the Space Rangers but heard of them over drinks in various bars. A planet which did not evolve and stayed in the Jurassic age. *Which means Sal could have more problems than I suspected,* she thought. Sal might be running for her life from big, sharp, reptilian teeth.

"Honestly," Nat answered. "It may be a dinosaur planet, which means we need to find Sal sooner rather than later." She reached for the dash and typed in a set of codes to activate the ship's sonar. It was old school and rarely used, but the technology would scan for sound blips radiating from honing beacons. It was amazingly acute and could target even the smallest pulse. Considering the dinosaurs and what was likely a lack of any technology, Nat felt the sonar option was an excellent way to search. It seemed unlikely there would be a lot of machinery with beacons activated. As she started to explain all that to Catherine, her idea paid off. A steady blip came from not more than a hundred miles to their south. Turning the ship, Nat swooped in that direction and covered the distance within a minute. As they neared the signal, she noted they were crossing over a giant lake. *What in the heck is transmitting this blip?* she thought. Water covered the whole area.

"Is it coming from here?" Catherine asked, and Nat knew the young woman was puzzled by the landscape as well. "What could possibly be here?" Nat did not have an answer, but she lowered their altitude until they skimmed the water. The blip grew stronger, and when they neared one edge of the lake, Nat saw her answer. There was the outline of a submerged starship.

The water was amazingly clear, and she made out the features of the craft. It was a Space Ranger starship. If she had to guess, Sal arrived on the planet with it, but now the question was if Sal was still aboard.

"She's not on there," Catherine insisted. "Sal would never let that happen to her, and you know it." Nat tilted her head, having to agree. If Sal knew she was about to crash into the lake, she would eject from the starship. More than likely there was no one aboard the craft. Still, she scanned with infrared and wished for a minute Catherine was not sitting beside her, just in case. As they skimmed over the submerged starship, Nat let out a breath of relief. There was no clear sign anything human-size was in the water. As she started to pull up, she noticed a large shape suddenly appear.

"What the hell is that?" she muttered, looking at the sensor while the shape grew near. At the last second, she looked at the windshield, in time to see a creature the size of a school bus, break the surface and lunge in their direction. Its jaws were wide. "My God," Catherine gasped. Nat responded by pulling back on the joystick, barely lifting the craft beyond the reach of the snapping teeth. It was closer than she thought it would be considering the size of the creature. The thing gained a lot more height out of the water than she anticipated. *Let's hope Sal managed not to get eaten by that*, Nat thought and hoped Catherine did not come to the same conclusion. Increasing their elevation and moving away from the lake, Nat returned to scanning for beacon pulses.

"Was that a giant crocodile?" Catherine asked.

Nat nodded. "Are you okay?" she asked, cruising the tops of the trees yet again.

"I think so," Catherine answered in a whisper. "Poor Sal."

Nat sighed. Things did not look good. Without a spaceship, there would be no easy way to send a signal. *And surviving this planet at all seems more impossible by the second*, she thought. Still, it was Salishan Bransen. "Baby, you said yourself, if anyone can make it, it will be Sal," she reassured Catherine. "We will keep—" She cut off her words when a very faint blip started on the furthest corner of the radar. Considering she had nothing else to hone in on, Nat turned them in that direction. *If Sal's starship was in the lake, what can this be?*

"What is it? Another ship?" Catherine asked. Nat was not sure. She sensed this was an extremely rudimentary environment. Still, she could not deny something sent off a wave her sonar picked up. Wanting an explanation, Nat raced in that direction. After a few kilometers, she noticed a strange object sticking out of the top of the canopy of trees. Blinking as she tried to comprehend what she saw, Nat slowed their progress.

"Catherine, do you see what I'm seeing?" she asked. Catherine got up and came closer, leaning toward the windshield to stare out.

"It looks like the tail of a giant spaceship," Catherine murmured. "Like, a really old one. Maybe it crashed?"

Nat nodded. It did look like an Esla Galaxy Cruiser from long ago. An original exploration model.

"This is it. Sal is down there," Catherine said. Nat raised an eyebrow at the conviction in Catherine's voice. *What about this relic of the spaceship makes her think it has anything to do with Sal's location?* she wondered. Regardless, it warranted checking out, and she lowered their ship until they hovered to the side of the tail of the starship. Switching back to the infrared to detect heat signatures, she was surprised by the results. At the base of where she estimated the starship's nose was planted there were dozens of tiny shapes. *And two larger ones.* Excited, Catherine clapped her hands and Nat grinned.

"I do believe you may be right," Nat said. Something told her the largest shape moving around under the trees was none other than Salishan Bransen.

CHAPTER 31
JADE

When Jade heard the sound of the starship hovering over their location, she was nothing less than shocked. It was true Sal sent off a distress call before they jumped into hyperdrive. Sal even seemed convinced something would come of it, but Jade put little stock in anyone helping them. Never in a million years did she think whoever received the message would react, especially so quickly. *This could make for an interesting situation*, Jade thought watching Sal as she turned her eyes toward the sky. A grin like Jade never saw on the woman's features before broke out across Sal's face. "That's them," Sal said and glanced at Jade.

Jade nodded. "Incredible," she murmured checking for markings on the spaceship above. *Not a Space Ranger craft*, she thought with a hint of relief. *Something privately owned. A Verado maybe?* "Your plan with the beacon worked." From the beginning, Jade went along with Sal's idea of searching the giant wreck of a galaxy cruiser to try and find a signaling device. In her heart, she thought the enterprise was a waste of time, and after searching the entire ship, including the transformer room that powered the entire craft, she was convinced she was right.

There was nothing with life left in it. Sal was diligent though and tried every control, and every power source, but nothing worked. When they finally reached the captain's bridge, all the consoles were dark and corroded after decades of sitting. Still, Sal tried all the devices. Finally, the woman stood from where she kneeled under a console checking wires and looked about ready to start kicking the place apart. Instead, she puffed out a frustrated breath. "That's that," she muttered turning to go and nearly tripped over the alien who helped them escape from the dinosaurs. She did not notice him in her frustration.

"Hey buddy," Sal said by way of apology. The little alien man stared up into her face as if he understood the words, then smiled as he held out his fist.

Jade moved closer. "Is everything okay?" she asked. He answered by turning his hand palm up and opening it. Jade held her breath when she recognized a small but potent battery source. It was precisely what Sal needed to fire up a distress beacon.

"Well, would you look at that. Been holding out on me?" Sal asked but with a hint of a smile. "What do you say we plug that baby in and see if anyone's nearby?"

Apparently, someone was listening, and it appeared escaping from the planet was not going to be Jade's biggest problem. As the sound of the starship started to fade, definitely moving in the direction of the big grass field, Sal waved Jade to follow. "Let's go," Sal said. "In case they attracted any predators."

Jade's mind raced through all the different scenarios she was likely to face when they reached the new arrivals. She had no idea who was landing. "Who do you think it is?" Jade asked as she hustled along trying to keep up with Sal's longer stride.

The woman was very eager to get to the field. Hearing chirping behind her, Jade looked over her shoulder and saw several aliens from the tribe followed in their footsteps. It was going to be quite a welcome committee.

"If I'm not mistaken, and I'm pretty sure I'm not, that starship is being piloted by none other than Captain Nat Reynolds of the 8th Galaxy Space Rangers.

"A Space Ranger?" Jade asked, slowing her steps. The last thing she wanted was to face a Space Ranger right now. *And why would a Space Ranger be coming to help Sal anyway? There must be some history there*, she thought and did not like the sound of it. "And how do you know this person?"

"It's complicated," Sal answered reaching the edge of the field. Jade saw the starship slowly settling onto the ground flattening the tall grass in a wide circle around it. "Let's just say we had a bit of an adventure together not too long ago. And the woman owes me a favor."

As they made their way toward the ship, Jade watched the gangway drop, and after a pause, a tall woman with light colored hair and broad shoulders stepped out. There was a look of authority about her as she came down the ramp. "I knew it," Sal said. "Her honor is too thick for her not to pay a debt." Jade thought it was an unusual thing to say considering she knew Sal put such little stock in honor. Still, there was clearly a bond between the two women.

As Sal walked toward the Ranger, Jade noticed another woman come through the spaceship's door. The Space Ranger paused to wait for her, and Jade could not help but see her beauty was breathtaking even from a distance. *Are they a couple then?* she wondered. *Why else bring her? Unless she's somehow connected to Sal?* It was all rather confusing, and only one thing was clear to Jade. The arrival of these two new people was not what she needed, but the spaceship was another story. *It does give me the opportunity to fly off of this rock.*

"Certainly took you long enough," Sal grumbled closing the distance to the couple waiting at the end of the gangway. Jade saw the light-haired woman scowl, but before she could make a retort, the younger woman stepped between them throwing her arms around Sal's neck to pull her into a hug.

"I'm so glad you're okay," she said. "We were so worried."

"What for?" Sal asked. "I'm fine."

The young woman pushed back from Sal and playfully slapped her on the shoulder. "You don't have to play all tough with me," she said. "I'm glad you had the sense to send a message to Nat so we could come to save you."

"Oh, so you think that's why I sent the message?" Sal asked with a smirk. "Maybe I wanted to show you this lovely planet."

"Lovely all right," the tall woman replied. "We were about chomped in half by a giant crocodile out over the lake, where you decided to land. Brilliant move, by the way."

"You don't know shit," Sal shot back. "It was land there or—"

Before Sal could finish her insult, the young woman put her hands up to stop the two women's bickering. "Enough," she said. "I'm not going to put up with this for the entire trip back to Untas."

Jade stiffened. Untas was the last place she wanted to go. As much as she needed to get off this dinosaur planet, she did not want to go back to the Space Ranger Base at Untas or at least not until she could take care of her primary objective. Suddenly, an idea struck her. She could solve two problems at once, and she did her best to hide a smile. It was good she did because at that moment Sal glanced over. For a moment it seemed Sal was reading her face, and their eyes held.

"Everything okay?" Sal asked, and Jade laughed.

"Could not be better," she replied honestly. "Now, introduce me to your friends."

Sal paused another second, but then let it go and turned to the young woman. "Jade, may I introduce Catherine Porter," Sal said. "No relation to the senator." This comment made the young girl laugh, and Jade looked from one to the other not understanding the joke. After a moment, the girl shook her head and stepped over holding out a hand in greeting.

"It's a pleasure to meet you, Jade," Catherine said. Jade took her hand, finding it gentle and warm. There was a certain grace about the woman even though it was clear she was probably not even twenty yet. *Beauty and confidence*, she thought. *A lethal combination.*

"Likewise," Jade replied and then turned her attention to the tall Ranger. The woman stepped forward and shook Jade's hand as well.

"Captain Nat Reynolds," she said. "I'm assuming we have you to thank for keeping Sal in one piece."

"Nobody had to keep me in one piece," Sal said with a hint of warning in her voice. Jade watched Nat bristle at the comment and start to turn. It was clear another verbal sparring match was about to begin. *These two really don't like each other*, Jade thought. *And yet they almost banter like siblings.* It was all such a strange circumstance but not one she cared to find out more about. What she wanted was to find a way to slip past all

of them and get on that ship. Jade was not familiar with the Verado series but knew she would figure it out. There was no alternative. Getting into the cockpit with the coder undetected
would be the tricky part. Regardless, the starship was her ticket
out of here, and she had no intention of taking any of the other
three humans with her. There was more than one way to complete her mission.

CHAPTER 32
CATHERINE

Catherine sat with the others around a firepit at the center of the alien village and discretely watched the interactions between Sal and Jade Hamilton. Back at the clearing when they first met, Sal introduced the woman in an offhanded way, basically saying she was the person who "got them into this mess" and no more was discussed. Later, she learned Jade was also a Space Ranger and the agent in charge of the mission gone bad. Jade made it quite clear the relationship was purely professional. Still, as Catherine watched them together tonight, she was confident there was an attraction there. On Jade's part at least. *How is that a surprise?* Catherine thought. *After all, it is Sal and who doesn't think she is intriguing?* With a smile, she refocused on trying to eat the mystery meat on her plate. She was pretty sure she did not want to know the source of the meal. It certainly was not chicken.

Cutting off a small piece, she slipped it into her mouth and went back to studying Jade while she chewed. The woman was a pretty blonde, seemed smart, and was undoubtedly quite dangerous if she was a Space Ranger. In Catherine's experience, anyone who survived the Space Ranger Academy was a bit of badass at some level. Still, she got a different vibe from Jade. *More cunning?* Definitely less brute strength than Nat and Sal. *Not that she probably isn't quite deadly in her own right.*

As if feeling her gaze, Jade looked from where she sat beside Sal. Their eyes met and, at first, the woman seemed perturbed by the scrutiny, but then recovered and smiled. Catherine was not sure what to make of it. *Have I done something to offend her?* Catherine wondered. Regardless, Sal did not notice any of it as she was engaged in conversation with Nat about their current situation.

"So, let me see if I understand this one more time," Catherine heard Nat say with a hint of humor in her voice. "You were captured by her." Nat pointed at Jade.

Catherine saw Sal's color rise even beneath her olive skin. Nat's comment struck home, and she knew at any second Sal would throw back a retort. This went on pretty much since they landed, and Catherine was done putting up with it. "I'm sure there are extenuating circumstances," Catherine interjected, holding up a hand to silence Sal. A hint of something dangerous flickered in Sal's eyes but then was gone. Catherine was aware she was quite possibly the only person in the galaxy who could make Sal stop doing anything. Catherine did not know what it was about her holding power over the amazing woman, but someday she hoped she could find out. It was her wish they would someday have time to sit down and discuss it all. She was no fool. There was no doubt Sal was attracted to her, but it was different, not like it was with Nat. The feeling she sensed with Sal was more wistful. There were times even when something in Sal's eyes made Catherine think maybe the woman was not seeing her at all. *Perhaps someone from her past?* Catherine wondered. She looked forward to the day she could ask Sal about it.

"Let's get back on topic," Sal said.

Catherine gave her a grateful smile. "Yes, let's," she said. "Is it true the entire 8th Galaxy is searching for you thinking you are an assassin?"

Sal shrugged. "It's true," she answered.

"In that case, please tell me you had some glimmer of a plan before you sent me a message," Nat growled.

Sal shot her a look. "I always have a plan," she countered.

"Well then, let's hear it," Nat said. "And it better not involve you and I going in somewhere, guns blazing, like the last time. I nearly lost a leg. God knows what will happen to me this time."

Catherine sighed knowing at this rate the discussion would take most the night. It seemed every comment was going to have some barb attached. *If only they could realize how alike there are*, Catherine thought before standing to move to the edge of the firepit.

She knelt next to one of the alien women who was stoking the flames, and Catherine smiled at her. "Thank you for dinner," Catherine said. The alien stared at her confused. Wanting to make herself understood, Catherine mimed eating and rubbed her tummy. That brought a laugh from the alien woman, but with good humor, and Catherine was confident she understood. She even patted Catherine on the shoulder in a maternal way that made Catherine a little homesick. Her parents, after being reunited six months ago, renewed their wedding vows, and then went on a prolonged honeymoon. It seemed Catherine's mother, before being captured, invested a few credits. A dozen years of earnings, while she was in the captivity of the space pirates, added up. Not an outlandish amount of credits, but it was enough for her parents to live comfortably and take a lavish vacation to celebrate finding each other again.

Happy for them but looking forward to when she could see them again, Catherine did not notice someone come up beside her. The sudden presence gave her a start, and she looked over to see Jade. "So how do you know Sal and Nat?" the woman asked as she knelt beside her. Catherine thought the comment was meant to be conversational, but there was a slight edge. She wondered if Jade was a little jealous. *Apparently, she does have feelings for Sal*, Catherine thought, but for some reason felt it was a bad thing. She tilted her head and considered Jade for a moment before answering. She did not know the woman, but she instinctively did not trust her. *But that's not fair. I have nothing to hold against her besides her involvement in Sal's predicament, which sounds like was out of her control.* Catherine was well accustomed to the Space Ranger way of things, and Jade was no doubt following orders. After living with Nat, she knew, for a Space Ranger, there was no alternative but to obey.

"We met when Nat and I were on our way to see my aunt on the planet Untas," Catherine answered. "Sal is one of the space pirates who intercepted our spaceship and kidnapped us."

Jade raised her eyebrows. "Really?" she asked. "So, you are the one."

Catherine forced a laugh, not sure she appreciated Jade's tone. "What does that mean?" she asked.

Jade smiled shaking her head. "Well, there was talk a damsel in distress triggered the downfall of the space pirate hideout. I did not realize I was in the presence of someone so special," she answered in a tone which was no doubt meant to sound playful but fell flat. There was a trace of meanness to it.

Catherine kept her voice even. "I had not heard that," she said. "But if I was in any way instrumental in setting so many slaves free, including my mother, I am happy."

"Your mother?" Jade asked with a furrowed brow. "What does that mean?"

Catherine waved a hand. "It's a long story," she replied, standing up. "I think we should go back and see how Sal and Nat are getting along. They may need a referee." Without waiting for Jade, she turned to leave the fire.

"Actually," Jade said suddenly standing so close to Catherine their shoulders almost brushed. "I think I need a favor from you."

"A favor?" Catherine asked instinctively not liking the sound of it. *What can this woman possibly need from me?* she wondered. Then, Jade revealed a knife from behind her back. With a cruel smirk, Jade pointed the blade at Catherine's side.

"I need you to convince your sweetheart to hand over the FSD coder for her fancy starship," Jade said.

Catherine was confused. "Why does that require you putting a knife on me?" Catherine asked getting over her surprise and becoming angry. "If you need something, ask. Nat will help you find whatever it is."

"That's just it," Jade said. "And I don't expect you to get it, being some naïve young girl who somehow landed a handsome Space Ranger, but I don't want anyone to accompany me onto the starship. It's time for me to get off of this godforsaken planet. Alone."

"What the hell are you doing?" Catherine heard Sal say with a growl. Turning to look, Catherine saw Sal and Nat were up from where they sat and staring at Catherine and Jade. "You have about three seconds to throw the knife on the ground, Jade," Sal continued. "Before I snap your neck."

CHAPTER 33
SAL

Sal stilled her body but could not stop the racing of her heart as she stared at Jade holding a knife against Catherine. Her threat was real. Sal was going to kill Jade if it was the last thing she ever did. There was always something about the woman which kept Sal from becoming more involved with her. All the opportunities to have sex with her and yet, strangely, Sal had resisted. As if some instinct inside her, those instincts which she always trusted entirely, knew this day would come. Jade would turn against her and show her true colors. All Sal wondered next was how deep her involvement in the setup went.

Out of the corner of her eye, Sal saw Nat start to shift to her right ever so slowly. *She wants to flank her*, Sal thought. It was precisely the kind of move she would make, too. Sal would keep Jade's attention while Nat was in a position to disarm her. Unfortunately, Jade was not a rookie, but an experienced agent and she noticed Nat. "One more step, Captain, and your woman will have a hole in her." Sal watched as Nat stopped, her body stiffening. The fury radiating from her was almost palpable. As much as Sal knew she hated the idea of Catherine being in the grasp of someone who meant to do her harm, it would not compare to what Nat felt.

"Choose your next move wisely," Nat spat, hands clenched into fists.

Jade lifted her chin. "Let me make this clear," she said. "I want the coder to the starship, and I want it now. Or I kill Catherine."

"You won't do it," Nat said, and Sal wondered if that was the best threat. Jade may very well do such a desperate thing.

"Actually, I would be happy to," Jade answered with a smirk. "The way the two of you moon over her is almost disgusting. But luckily, it is those emotions which make me confident you both will go along with what I say."

Sal paused as she considered Jade's words. *Am I acting toward Catherine as Jade suggests?* she wondered. *Is she my weakness?* Sal was not sure of the answers. Catherine was important to her. So much so, at one point it kept her from ravishing the woman back at the pirate hideaway. *What is it about her I can't deny? A gentle soul? Beautiful brown-eyes?* The same attributes as another girl Sal remembered all too well. They were teenagers together. *So long ago.* With a shake of her head to refocus on the situation at hand, Sal banished those memories as she had a hundred times before. What was done, was done.

"I'm going to give you until the count of three," Jade warned. "And then I guarantee you things will start to happen. Now give me the coder."

"I agree," Sal said. "Things will definitely start to happen." Her words were not a threat, but a promise. If Jade cut even one hair on Catherine's head, she would enjoy killing Jade using every bit of torture she learned with the space pirates.

"Nat," Catherine said. "Don't do it. I don't know what's going on here, but don't let her bluff you."

"I assure you, little miss," Jade growled. "This is not a bluff."

Sal watched as Nat pulled the coder for the starship out of her pocket and tossed it on the ground at Jade's feet. "Take it," she spat. "Now let her go."

"That's better," Jade said, and Sal watched her press the point of the knife harder into Catherine's side. The woman flinched, and Sal took a step forward. "Don't Sal," Jade warned and then let out a spiteful laugh. "You got it bad for her, don't you?"

For the first time, Sal noticed there was a hint of envy in the woman's eyes. *Because she knows she will never compare to Catherine,* Sal thought. Although there was undeniable chemistry between her and Jade from the beginning, it was strictly physical. The lust was the reason why Jade was able to capture her in the beginning. For Sal though, it was nothing more than that. Jade would be nothing but another conquest. *It does not appear to have been going both ways,* Sal thought realizing more was going on with Jade than she ever realized. *And why is that?* They hardly knew each other.

Just then, Jade started to lean down to pick up the coder. As she did, Catherine grabbed the knife and pushed away from it. "No," Sal exclaimed and leaped forward. Jade was too fast, and she swiped out with the blade. Moving in what felt like slow motion, Sal's worst fears were realized as Catherine went spinning away from the thrust and fell to the ground. For a moment, Sal was conflicted. She wanted both to tackle Jade and check Catherine. Nat helped her make up her mind as, in an instant, the Space Ranger was past Jade and at Catherine's side.

Moving in a blur, Sal grasped Jade around the throat and forced her to the ground. She leaned in, with a knee in her chest, with every intention of killing the woman. The only thing stopping her from snapping the woman's neck like a twig was a desire for answers. All this was the dealing of some sort of master plan. *But who's plan?* she wondered. *And to what purpose?* Jade was possibly the only person who would have the answers, and it was the only thing keeping her alive.

"How is she?" Sal asked without looking over, still staring into Jade's face which was slowly growing blue. Answers or no answers, if Catherine was gone Jade would be as well.

"I'm okay," Catherine answered, and Sal felt the band around her chest lessen. *She's okay,* Sal thought letting the words ripple through her.

"Yes," Nat agreed. "A minor flesh wound. Catherine moves faster than we thought." There was a touch of humor and relief in Nat's voice, and Sal let herself relax a breath further. "Don't kill her," Nat continued. "I would like to know what the hell is going on."

Sal agreed, slowly releasing the pressure on the woman's neck. Jade gasped, sucked in a lungful of air, and turned her head to retch in the dirt. *I was closer to killing her than I thought.* The rage coursing through her gave her greater strength than she realized. "You are lucky to be alive," Sal growled. "Remember that." Jade nodded but continued to cough.

While Jade struggled on the ground, clearly not going anywhere anytime soon, Sal turned her attention to Catherine. She was still sitting on the ground as well. Sal ran her eyes down the woman's body and saw traces of blood on her shirt. She watched as Catherine hiked up her fabric as the old woman alien joined them and motioned toward the wound. Sal looked around and only now noticed the members of the tribe were coming out of hiding. *Smart enough to get out of any crossfire*, Sal thought with respect. She turned her attention back to the old woman realizing she held a clay pot in her hands. Leaning closer, Sal was able to see there was a salve in it and when the woman nodded towards Catherine's side, Sal guessed it was some type of medicinal ointment. The alien held it out to Nat and, when she took it, the woman made a rubbing motion.

"Rub it on her cut?" Nat asked. The alien nodded making more rubbing motions. Nat glanced at Sal. "What do you think?"

"I imagine it will work better than anything we have," Sal answered. "These folks look healthy considering they are probably pretty low on the food chain on this particular planet."

"Okay," Nat said, putting two fingers into the ointment before rubbing it on Catherine's side.

"Oh, that's cool. Nice. It is already taking away the pain," Catherine said. Satisfied the woman was going to be okay, Sal turned her attention back to Jade, who had returned to a normal color and looking around as if she could escape.

"You don't seriously think you can make it to the trees before I kill you?" Sal asked.

Jade's shoulders sank. "No," she answered not meeting Sal's eyes.

"You ready to explain where the hell you thought you were going on the starship?" Sal asked.

Jade shrugged. "Back," she said.

"Back where?" Sal asked feeling her temper rising again. She was never a fan of torturing Space Rangers while she was with the space pirates, but she had every intention of getting answers out of Jade.

"Untas," Jade finally answered as if sensing what was on Sal's mind. "To report the mission was successful."

Sal nodded. "Successful as in I'm dead?" she asked.

Jade blew out a breath and paused before answering. "Yes."

CHAPTER 34
NAT

Nat felt Catherine's warmth as she snuggled against her. For a moment, she was not sure where they were because a second before she was dreaming of the Royal Venus Hotel—a place they stayed months ago, and where they first got to know each other. Opening her eyes, Nat realized they were on the Verado starship, and the memory of Catherine's injury from last night flooded back. Slowly, she rolled over to avoid disturbing the sleeping woman and was relieved to see no look of pain on her face. The salve the aliens gave them did wonders, not only taking away the pain, but speeding up the healing process. Nat intended to take a sample of the miracle cure back with her. Although they were not able to get great answers from the aliens of the source, with the limited vocabulary between them, one of the males lead them to a tall tree and pointing at the leaves. Nat gathered a few and photographed the tree as well.

Resting while studying Catherine's beautiful face, Nat felt relief like never before. The woman who she loved so much, when she fell, Nat feared the worst. *If something truly happened to her...* Nat thought and closed her eyes to ward off the pain at the very idea. *If something happened to her, I would never forgive myself for bringing her along. And I don't think I could live without her.* The last thought surprised Nat. *Are my feelings so deep for this woman I genuinely do not know if I could survive should Jade have killed her?* Nat took a deep breath. Yes, Catherine was her everything. She opened her eyes to gaze at Catherine's face.

As if hearing her thoughts and feeling the tenderness in her heart, Catherine blinked her eyes open and looked into Nat's face. Noticing Nat watching, Catherine smiled. "How long have you been awake?" she asked.

Nat returned the smile trying to mask the intensity of her emotions, and leaned to kiss Catherine on the forehead. "Long enough to appreciate your beauty," she answered. "Are you still hurting?"

Catherine paused, and Nat could tell she was taking stock of her body. After a moment she gave a slight shake of her head. "I hardly feel any irritation at all. I have to say, whatever the aliens gave us is a miracle," she said. Nat nodded, unable to form the words to describe her relief. Catherine's face became tender as she recognized the worry in Nat's eyes. "I'm sorry I scared you," she said. "But I couldn't let that woman get away with our starship and leave us stranded on this planet. I had to do something."

Nat let out a slow breath to keep her frustration over Catherine's actions to herself. What she did was quite brave, and Nat appreciated it, but still, she wanted the woman to be safe. Always. "I understand," she said. "But I hate it when you put yourself in harm's way." *Because I need you*, Nat thought realizing the truth. *If she is so important, I need to marry her.* Taking Catherine's face in her hands, Nat kissed the woman's lips tenderly. The words of a proposal were on the tip of her tongue when there was a knock at the starship's outside door.

"Wake the hell up in there," Nat heard Sal yell. "There's no time to waste, sleeping beauties." Nat grit her teeth. Leave it to Salishan Bransen to interrupt something so important. Nat realized with a growl she would need to wait until there was a better time to tell Catherine what was in her heart and ask her to be her wife.

"Hold your horses," Nat yelled back giving Catherine a peck on the lips, before rolling out of bed and pulling on her uniform pants. Another knock, more insistent this time, came from the door. Already Sal was getting under Nat's skin and the day was only beginning. The irritation was so much Nat was pretty sure the woman did it on purpose. "One more time," Nat warned. "I dare you." There was a long pause, but when Nat reached the door, there was a loud bang as if Sal kicked it. "You gotta be kidding me," Nat said under her breath and activated the device to whisk the door open.

Sal stood there next to Jade, whose hands were tied behind her back. "You are an inconsiderate son of a bitch," Nat said. "You want to tell me what the rush is?"

"Some of us have shit to get done today," Sal replied.

The sarcasm in Sal's voice grated on Nat to the point she marched down the gangway to come to a stop within a foot of Sal. They were the same height and stared into each other's eyes. Nat's eyes were blue, and her hair was blonde while Sal's hair and eyes were brown. Catherine told her once she thought they were two sides of the same coin—one light and one dark. Nat never understood it, knowing there was nothing similar about them. Nat had honor, and she was brave. Sal only thought of herself and was more reckless. "You need to shut up," Nat warned.

Sal smirked. "Well, obviously, you haven't brushed your teeth yet," Sal said. "So, unless you're about to give me a kiss, back the fuck up." Nat balled her hands into fists, every cell in her body wanted to knock Sal on her ass. Suddenly from behind her, she heard movement on the gangway.

"Nat, please stop," she heard Catherine ask. "The two of you need to figure this out. But this is not the way to do it." Nat slowly let her hands relax and took a step back. Sal continued to smirk, but Nat chose to ignore it for now and turned to hold out a hand to Catherine. Catherine moved closer and took it. The warmth of her soft hand further calmed Nat's anger. When the young woman smiled and mouthed "thank you" Nat knew her actions were the right ones.

"So, what is your big plan?" Nat asked looking back at Sal. She noticed Sal relaxed significantly as well. It was as if Catherine held a way of calming rough waters for them both.

"For starters, we need to lock Jade up in the bathroom on the starship. Putting her in a holding cell on the galaxy cruiser was fine overnight, but I want to take her back with us, and I'm tired of babysitting her," Sal said. "She has ever so kindly *volunteered* to help us get back to Untas and arrange a meeting with Petrus Cunningham."

Nat was surprised and raised her eyebrows. "Petrus Cunningham? The 8th Galaxy Chief of Staff? she asked. "Why?"

Sal turned her gaze to stare at Jade who responded with a glare of her own. "Because even though Jade has yet to confirm it, I can feel in my gut he is the mastermind behind all this. I'd like to have a conversation," Sal said.

Nat looked at Jade, took in her stubborn features, and decided she was probably the last person who was going to cooperate. Nat pointed at her. "And she's going to help us?" Nat said, skepticism in her voice.

"She will," Sal answered. "Or I will teach her special things I learned from the space pirates."

Nat did not care for the sound of that threat. She heard rumors over the years of what the space pirates did to Space Rangers', and it made her stomach clench. *Let it go*, Nat thought. *As Catherine so often says, now is not the time.*

CHAPTER 35
CATHERINE

Catherine was ready for them to depart. She was eager to fly back to civilization, help Sal clear her name, and put that matter to rest. She knew it weighed heavily on both Nat and Sal. As Space Rangers or in Sal's case ex-Space Ranger, reputations were important and knowing most of the 8th Galaxy was looking for them as fugitives made them both somber. She knew Sal tried to pretend none of it mattered to her, that she was willing to live her life as an outlaw, but Catherine perceived slight cracks in her armor. Although she would never be free of the fear the space pirates would come after her again, being unwelcome everywhere would be too much. In her heart, Catherine was not convinced Sal could be satisfied with never having some sort of normal life. *And I hope somehow Nat and I are part of it*, she thought as they reached the gangway of the Verado spaceship.

They had spent the morning thanking their alien hosts for all the help and hospitality. After an exchange of gifts, which luckily Nat dug up from the limited inventory on the starship, they were finally ready. Or so she thought, until both Nat and

Sal made a move to enter the cockpit. "Where do you think you're going?" Nat asked Sal.

"The pilot's seat," Sal said, a touch of irritation in her voice. "Obviously." Catherine froze. She never considered this possibility. Both women were amazing pilots, and therefore both women would expect to fly the spaceship.

"That's not going to happen," Nat replied. "Now, go relax in the back." Slowly Sal turned to face Nat until they were nose-to-nose. Catherine held her breath.

"You know I am the better pilot," Sal said. "Don't be an asshole about this." Catherine saw Nat's eyebrows shoot up.

"Me be an asshole?" she said. "You've got to be kidding. We came here, risking our lives, to save you and now you're trying to give me this crap?"

"Save me?" Sal said the return. "I needed a lift. Besides, I think you forget not too long ago who was saving who." Catherine knew she needed to get between them or at any minute this would escalate and be out of control.

"Please, you two," she said. "Stop this. We have other things more important to think about." For a second, she thought they would both relent and listen to her wise words. Then, she saw Nat lift her chin and knew there would be trouble. Her lover was the most caring and gentle woman she ever met. She was brave, and she was strong, but she was also stubborn. Having seen the look on her face before, Catherine knew Nat was thinking of her honor. There was no way she was going to let Sal fly them anywhere. Moving her gaze to look at Sal, Catherine was not surprised to see the same look there.

"I think it's time we settled this once and for all," Nat said in a low voice. "Let's step outside, shall we?"

"Oh yeah," Sal chuckled. "Bring it on."

"No," Catherine said with as much authority she could muster. "We are not going to do this."

Slowly Nat held up her hand as if to ward off Catherine's advice. "Catherine, my love, some things are handled a certain way," she said. Catherine's hopes fell when she saw Sal give one quick nod.

"Exactly," Sal agreed and waved for Nat to lead the way back out the door and down the gangway. Catherine could do nothing but follow as the two women walked into the field of trampled grass surrounding the ship. Stopping at the end of the gangway, Catherine opened her mouth to try and talk reason again. As she did, she saw Nat and then Sal stop. To her shock, when Nat turned back to face Sal, the woman lashed out with astonishing speed. It was a blur and Catherine could not utter a sound before Sal's fist struck Nat hard in the cheekbone. The blow rocked Nat, but for a moment Catherine thought she might stay upright. Then, her knees bent, and she went down. *Cheap shot!* Catherine thought, her temper rising. They should have known Sal, after all her years of living the pirate's life, would have no druthers about winning a fight that way.

Shaking her head with anger, Catherine started down the gangway to go to Nat's side. As Sal turned toward her and began to walk back to the ship, Catherine threw herself in the woman's path. She put a finger in the middle of Sal's chest and glared up into the woman's face. "Sal, how could you?" Catherine asked. "Nat is—" Then, out of the corner of her eye, she saw Nat climbing to her feet. Surprised, considering how hard the blow looked, Catherine stopped. Curious, Sal glanced back to follow her gaze. The look on Sal's face was nothing less than astonishment. If Catherine could read her mind, she would guess Sal never thought in a million years anyone would get up so soon after that punch.

Suddenly, Nat was in motion. "Catherine, get out of the way," she roared. It was all Catherine could do to get back up the gangway as the woman moved with an astonishing speed of her own. Sal started to react but was not quick enough before Nat bull rushed her with all her force. She wrapped her arms around Sal's chest, lifting her, only to piledrive her into the dirt.

As Sal landed flat on her back with Nat on top, there was a look on Sal's face Catherine never saw before. It was surprise. *Could it be the great warrior and Ranger Salishan Bransen was rarely knocked on her back?* Catherine thought. *Especially by someone she laid out with a sucker punch.* Catherine felt a twinge of pride knowing her woman was an equal match. *But where can this end?*

Biting her lip, she considered trying to get between them, to make them listen, but before she could act, Sal pulled her legs up under Nat and used them to lift the woman up and over her head. Nat went sprawling, but in an instant, they both jumped to their feet, facing off. "You sucker punched me," Nat said spitting onto the ground. "I should've known better."

Sal snorted a laugh. "Yes, you should have," she said. "I'm not like you, Captain. With all your honor and bullshit." As if to punctuate the statement, Sal lashed out with a wicked sidekick aimed at Nat's head. Nat ducked, but Catherine's eyes widened when the blow missed her by only a hair's breadth. Sal looked to be playing for keeps. She needed to find a way to stop this before one of them was hurt.

"You know what's bullshit?" Nat responded as the two women circled each other. "Your constant protest about not having any honor. Nobody believes you, Sal."

"Fuck off," Sal replied with a growl, while at the same time rushing Nat with a flying knee. The blow caught Nat in the chest, and Catherine let out a short scream, only to see her hero twist with the momentum to land a spinning back fist punch of her own. Sal danced away from the blow, but there was a line of blood over her left eye. Catherine saw her reach up and feel the cut, then look at her fingers. They were red. "Nice shot, Ranger," she admitted with a smirk. "Too bad it means now I'm going to—" Her words were cut off by a loud chirp coming from the direction of the alien village. All three of them turned to look, only to see one of the aliens waving his arms to get their attention. "Well, that can't be good," Catherine heard Sal mutter in the same instant a roar came from the jungle. Catherine's heart went cold. *What in the world was that?* she wondered. Her answer came barreling out of the wall of green surrounding the field.

"Catherine! Get back on the ship," Nat yelled, and Catherine started to back up the gangway but was unwilling to go inside without the other two women. Sal reached her first and started to turn her to go, but she resisted.

"No," she said, trying to push the much bigger woman out of the way. "We have to wait for Nat!"

"She's coming," Sal said, unwilling to move. "Now go."

As they struggled, Catherine watched Nat's progress through the tall grass. She was limping. *It's her bad knee*, she realized. *All the fighting made it act up.* To her horror, Nat stumbled, and the movement drew the dinosaur's attention. "Oh

God," she whispered and then pushed with all her strength to pass Sal. "Nat!" Sal held fast but glanced back. At that moment, Nat fell.

"Seriously," Catherine heard Sal growl. "Get inside, Catherine. I'll be right back." Then, the woman bolted down the gangway and back through the grass. Catherine held her breath as Sal reached Nat within seconds. Yanking her up, Sal slung Nat over her shoulder and turned to run back, but she was running out of time. The predator moved across the field at a run now. It bellowed a roar and Catherine knew the race would be a close one.

"Sal! Hurry," Catherine yelled. "It's coming!"

"Yeah, Sal, for Christ's sake hurry. It's right behind us," she heard Nat say a moment before the monster roared again.

"No shit, Sherlock. Get on the ship, Catherine" Sal yelled back. "Get ready to close the damn door." This time, Catherine obeyed and watched through the opening as Sal pumped her legs in a race for her life. The dinosaur drew closer, and as it opened its jaws to bite, Sal was on the gangway and diving through the door. "Close it!"

Catherine slammed her hand against the button to slide the door shut as Sal and Nat crashed in a heap on the floor. A pair of snapping jaws descended, and then the opening slipped closed. The entire spaceship rocked as the dinosaur slammed into the side. The roar of frustration rang through the air around them.

CHAPTER 36
SAL

Sitting in the pilot's chair, Sal held an icepack to her temple. They were out in space again, and she blew out a breath of relief. Finally, she could go looking for some answers.

"Ready for me to take a shift?" Nat asked from behind her. After untangling themselves on the floor while the dinosaur held a hissy-fit outside, Catherine explained they would be sharing the pilot duties, end of story.

Sal grit her teeth, not thrilled with the new arrangement, but let it go in the interest of keeping the peace, at least temporarily. "Yes," she said standing. "I need to get some pain killer for this headache anyway."

While Nat limped past and took over, she snorted a laugh. "Good luck with that. Meds are in the bathroom with Jade," she said. "That should be fun for you." Sal rolled her eyes but kept going. *It might be time to let Jade out of the bathroom anyway,* she thought. After all, the woman was in there for hours and probably more than a little pissed off about it.

Going to the door, Sal listened hearing nothing. *Sleeping?* she wondered. *Well, time to wakey-wakey.* Sal banged her fist against the door. A yip of surprise was her reward. "God-damnit," Jade muttered from behind the door. "Was that necessary?" Chuckling, Sal removed the knife she wedged through the door handle. It was just the ticket to jam the device that turned the lock. Sometimes a simple solution was the answer. Taking a step back, Sal reholstered the knife and waited. *Will she be bold enough to open the door without asking?* After a moment of no movement, Sal grinned. *Smart girl. Maybe she's not as bad as I thought.* It was entirely possible Jade was doing nothing more than saving her hide back there on the dinosaur planet, and not trying to kill Sal and the others. Sal appreciated making decisions which only benefited herself. She had been doing that for years. *Maybe it was not a double cross?*

"Come on out," Sal said stepping away when the door burst open. Jade came flying at Sal. Her hands were no longer bound, and she held a switchblade knife. With a yell of fury, Jade swung the blade at Sal. Unlike Nat though, Jade was slow enough Sal easily blocked her.

"Where in the hell did you have that thing hidden?" Sal asked as she grabbed the woman's wrist and easily plucked the blade from Jade's oncoming hand. After all, Sal searched her when she tied her up.

Thwarted, Jade harmlessly bounced off of Sal and went sprawling onto the bed in the small sleeping quarters beside the bathroom. "I'm sure you can imagine," Jade snarled, and Sal snorted a laugh.

"Well, I'll be. I'm impressed. Guess that teaches me a lesson," Sal said. "I should have had sex with you in the tree." She examined the knife for another moment before closing it and tucking the thing into her belt. Looking at Jade now, she was disgusted with herself. A minute ago, she was giving Jade the benefit of the doubt. *Letting my guard down yet again*, she thought. *What is it about this woman?*

Jade stared back at her. "Now what?" she asked, then her face softened. "You're hurt?" She started to get off the bed. "What happened?"

Sal shrugged. "I ran into Nat's fist," she said laughing at her humor. Jade shook her head, apparently confused.

"I don't understand," she said, and Sal waved her off.

"Forget about it," she said, but Jade started to get up, no doubt intending to nurture Sal.

"Let me help you," she said.

Furrowing her brow, Sal stared. "You can't be serious?" she asked. "After you tried to cut my throat?"

Jade sank back. "You know that was only out of survival. I still care for you," she said, but Sal was done buying her crap. In fact, her latest lie about wanting to help hurt a little, a sensation Sal was not used to feeling. Somehow, Jade got under her skin. With a shake of her head to try and dislodge whatever crazy thing was going on, Sal pulled a chair from the built-in desk in the corner of the room, turned it around, and straddled it. It was time to get down to facts with Jade. In that exact moment, Sal realized what it was about Jade which knocked her off balance. She reminded her of someone. Not from long ago, but more recent. *But who? A fellow Space Ranger? A space pirate?* she wondered. Sal spent a second wracking her brain trying to recall, but when it eluded her, she let it go. The memory would come to her eventually.

"So, let's talk," she said. "Now that you've had some time to think things over in the facilities, I imagine you're ready."

Jade shook her head. "I don't have anything new to add from what I explained last night. I panicked," she explained. "I wanted to go home."

Sal leaned back and tapped the side of the metal chair. This was the answer she expected and frankly was not in the mood to screw around torturing a different one out of her. "All right then, I guess you won't mind helping all of us get back to civilization again," she said. "And taking me to see the 8th Galaxy's Chief of Staff. I have a few things I want to say to Mr. Cunningham."

Jade's eyes widened almost imperceptibly, but Sal saw and knew that was the last thing Jade wanted to do. "I can't," she started.

Sal held up a hand to cut her off. When Jade stopped talking, Sal pulled the small switchblade Jade threatened her with earlier. She opened it, turned the weapon left and right to consider it. *Tiny, little bugger*, she thought, flicking the edge with her thumb, confirming it was razor sharp.

"Don't bother trying to convince me otherwise," Sal said. "If you can't get me to Petrus Cunningham, I have no use for you."

This time, Jade's eyes gave her away entirely. "You wouldn't ..." she whispered, but when Sal stood, Jade scooted back to the wall at the top of the bed.

"Trust me," Sal assured her. "I will. Pretty sure Nat will be pissed if I get blood all over her bed, but that almost makes it more fun." She took a step forward, raising the knife, when Catherine appeared in the doorway.

"Sal," she said alarm in her voice. "What are you doing?"

Crap, Sal thought, lowering the blade. She glanced at the young woman and noted her face was pale. "Just having a discussion with Jade," she answered. "I suggest you go to the cockpit with Nat. I'll only be a minute."

Catherine shook her head. "No, Sal, there has to be another way," she said, and Sal sighed. This was getting unnecessarily complicated.

"Was there something you needed?" Sal asked plastering a patient smile on her face.

Catherine narrowed her eyes. "Yes," she answered. "Nat says we are almost to the wormhole and we need a strategy to deal with the Space Ranger patrols." Catherine looked at Jade. "Perhaps you can help us with that?"

Sal looked at Jade noting the flickering emotions crossing her face. The woman was conflicted. "You have to have a passcode or special word to let the authorities know you've been successful," Sal said. "How about you go get on the commlink and square things away for all of us?"

Jade started shaking her head. "No," she said. "You saw. They were ready to kill me, too. Remember?"

Sal laughed. She did remember but was beginning to realize she was a bigger fool than she thought. *So, how elaborate was the setup after all?* she wondered. Before she responded to Jade's bullshit, Catherine stepped closer to Sal putting her hand on her shoulder. As always, the touch was warm and soothing. *She's going to try and talk me out of killing Jade.* Getting ready to form an argument, Sal was shocked by Catherine's nod.

"Then, she's worthless to us like you said, Sal," she murmured. "But please, can you try not to make a mess all over the bed?"

Sal heard Jade gasp. "Now wait," Jade started while Sal grinned. Catherine never ceased to surprise her.

"I'll be careful," she said at the same time Jade crawled closer already begging.

"I do know the code," she admitted. "I can get you to Petrus Cunningham. Whatever you need."

Sal narrowed her eyes as she considered the woman. It was possible this was another setup. *I have no radar with this one*, she thought. Deciding not to risk it, she turned to Catherine. "Well, what do you think?" she asked her. "Believe her?"

"It's true," Jade added, her voice rising. "I swear on my life. He set everything up. He wants to be president and needed a smokescreen. Everyone is focused on finding the assassin and not his take over. I can take you to him."

Sal watched Catherine slowly nod. "I do believe that," she said after a pause. "Okay, let's get her up front. Tied up again, of course."

"Absolutely," Sal agreed slipping the knife away. "I'm going to see the Chief of Staff again." She chuckled. "This will be fun."

CHAPTER 37

JADE

When Jade walked into Petrus Cunningham's office, with his receptionist panicking at her heels, she was thrilled by the look of utter surprise on the man's face. He clearly was not expecting her to show up, possibly ever again. The realization was enough to make Jade even more furious. Clenching her teeth to keep from giving away how much she despised the man, she strode across the floor to stop in front of his large, and no doubt expensive as hell, desk. "You look shocked," she said, keeping her voice even. "I told you from day one I would pull this mission off."

Suddenly, an armed Ferg bodyguard appeared through a side door, and she knew Cunningham must have pushed a silent alarm. *I can't say I blame him*, she thought. *I'd be nervous to see me.*

"I'm so sorry, sir," his receptionist whimpered. "She just—"

Cunningham waved her quiet regaining his composure once there was security in the room. "Go," he said. "And close the door." He turned his attention back to Jade narrowing his eyes. "How in the hell did you get this far into the building undetected?"

Jade smiled. "A woman has her ways," she answered. "But don't worry. I'm not armed. You can have your pet check if you want." Cunningham waved the bodyguard over, and Jade stood patiently while he patted her down. Stepping back, he gave his boss a nod and Jade watched the Chief of Staff relax even further, all the while keeping a disappointed frown on his face.

"Next time, make an appointment," he said. "But since you are here. What do you have for me?"

"A body you mean?" Jade replied taking joy in watching Cunningham squirm a little at her question. His guy was on a need to know only basis. "Oh, sorry," she continued winking at the bodyguard. "All in good fun. I'm sure you never guessed your boss was someone who would arrange for an assassination."

Cunningham shot out of his chair. "Jesus!" he exclaimed. "Have you lost your mind?"

Jade could not hold back a laugh now. "Oh, come on, Petrus," she said taking pleasure in using his first name. "I am sure your man won't breathe a word. And for the record, the answer is no. I do not have Salishan Bransen's body. I left her to rot on a dinosaur planet at the edge of the galaxy. Not a stitch of technology. No one will ever find her."

Slowly, Cunningham sank down nodding. "That will do. Quite well, actually," he said. "That way, if I ever need to hand her over to the space pirates, I know where she is."

Jade loved it. *I should have thought of that myself,* she thought. If only Catherine cooperated. Jade knew she was moments away from a clean getaway and then somehow it all fell apart. *But not this time...* Shaking her head to refocus on the moment, Jade stepped closer to the desk. "So, I do have one question," she said. "At what point did I become expendable in your little mission to become the next president of the 8th Galaxy?"

This remark landed like she hoped as Cunningham's face immediately flushed red. "Now wait a minute, enough is enough," he sputtered waving at his bodyguard to grab Jade. "I think it's time for you to go, agent."

Jade held up her hands in surrender. "Sorry, I'll go. But I'm expecting a hell of a payment for all of this," she said walking back to the door. "I went through a lot for you."

As she crossed the room, she was pleased to hear Cunningham agree. "You will be," he promised. "A job well done, Ranger."

It was enough for Jade, and she opened the door to let Sal walk in. The woman stepped forward with only a flicker of rage snapping in her dark eyes to give away how much she hated the man. *A deadly* look, Jade thought as she turned in time to see the bodyguard pull his plasma gun. She almost laughed knowing the Ferg had zero chance of getting the weapon up in time. Sal stunned him before he even made it halfway. Next, Sal turned her gun on Petrus, and the man raised his hands. "Now wait a minute—" he started, but Jade cut him off.

"Did you get it?" Jade asked Sal, and she nodded.

"Commlink recorded every word," she said crossing the room bearing down on a sputtering Petrus Cunningham. *At least he's not quaking like a coward*, Jade thought giving the man a point for having balls. *I guess you don't get to be the most powerful man in the galaxy otherwise.*

"Someone want to explain to me what in the fuck is going on?" he finally snapped doing an excellent job of looking angry even as Sal leveled the weapon in her hand at his head.

"Miss me?" she said with a smirk. Cunningham's eyes darted to Jade as if looking for help, but then jerked back to Sal.

Jade shrugged. "Don't look at me, Petrus," she said checking to see if Sal was still focused on Cunningham before moving to stand beside the unconscious bodyguard. Pleased the woman was distracted, Jade picked up the guard's plasma gun. "You did this to yourself. Seems Sal was a bad choice after all."

The man's face grew a deep shade of red. "She was your idea! You insisted we use her," he said, his voice rising an octave to show he was more upset than he appeared as the direness of the situation settled in. There was a moment when the room stilled as Jade watched Cunningham's last sentence register with Sal. Then the woman was turning, but this time Jade was ready, finger on the trigger of the bodyguard's gun.

"Move another hair Sal, and I'll gladly blow a hole in you," Jade said. "Go ahead. How fast are you?" Sal said nothing, and only stared into Jade's eyes. There was no hint of emotion there, and Jade was sick of it. *She has no idea who I am?* she thought. Even now. They went through so much together in such a short amount of time. The seduction at the bar, the chemistry, even Jade's betrayal failed to register.

Sal raised her eyebrows. "Do I at least get a hint?" she asked guessing there was some history she was not aware of between them.

Pleased the woman at least made that connection, Jade nodded. "Put down the weapon first," she said waiting as Sal casually tossed the thing over her shoulder where it bounced along the carpet.

"Okay, so now what?" Sal asked. If she was afraid of the plasma gun pointed at her, a person would never know it. As much as Jade did not want to admit the truth, it was hard not to be impressed by the ice in the woman's veins.

"You're quite a character, Salishan Bransen," she said. "But that does not make you less of a monster."

Sal slowly tilted her head, studying Jade's face. Another minute passed, and at last, Jade saw a glimmer of recognition. "Your sister was also a Space Ranger," Sal said. It was not a question. Clearly, Sal remembered something, and Jade hoped she finally realized how close she was to her last breath. "You look a lot like her."

"Yes," Jade agreed. "She was my older sister, but people often mistook us for twins."

Sal nodded. "I bet," she said. "And she was captured by the space pirates."

Jade tightened her grip on the plasma gun suddenly more ready than ever to kill the woman. There was nothing stopping her now. Only the desire for the truth kept her from pulling the trigger. "Oh, she was more than captured," Jade whispered. "She was tortured for information and left for dead on a scuttled space transport."

Jade watched Sal nod slowly looking into the distance as she called up the memory. "And you figure I had something to do with that business?" she asked, but Jade knew the woman was remembering. Jade's sister's last words were well documented. Sal had been her tormentor.

A tear slipped down Jade's cheek at the thought of it. "How could you? You were with the Corps, yet you willingly did those things to your fellow Rangers," Jade choked out.

Sal sighed. "It was complicated," she said, with what Jade realized was sincere remorse in her voice. "I promise you, I remember your sister. Her suffering was nothing compared to so many. I always tried to protect the women, although no one would ever know it. It's the only reason she was still alive at all." She looked back into Jade's eyes. "But maybe this is for the best. Go ahead. Shoot me, Jade."

Jade hesitated, not sure what to make of this change, and before she could recover, the door to the office burst open. Sal dove for her abandoned weapon and Jade, knowing her opportunity was slipping away, turned to fire.

CHAPTER 38
NAT

Nat called in every favor she stored up over the years as a Space Ranger to get permission to lead a squad of six Rangers into the office of the 8th Galaxy's Chief of Staff. Only by going as high as the director herself was Nat able to make it happen. She put her entire career on the line, and all she could hope was Sal's plan to wire Jade worked, and they had the confession recorded on a commlink.

With guns drawn, the team rushed the door and Nat took in the scene realizing things were definitely not going according to plan. Jade was about to fire on Sal who was making a dive toward a plasma gun in the corner. Nat watched as Sal landed hard, still facing away from Jade, and knew she would be too late to defend herself.

All in one instant, Nat moved like a flash to jump in front of Jade's line of fire as she drew down on the woman. "Hold your fire, agent," she barked while aiming.

The woman looked determined but hesitated. "Stay out of this," she said, hysteria in her voice. "Salishan Bransen deserves to die for all she has done."

"I won't ask you again," Nat barked keeping a bead on Jade. "Let the authorities handle this. Put down your weapon."

Jade shook her head. "No, she will escape again. She always does," she said, and Nat knew in her heart the woman was going to shoot. With no choice, Nat fired. The blast caught Jade in the chest and knocked her off her feet. The setting of Nat's gun was full stun, but the force was still significant, and Jade spun in the air before slamming into the floor.

Christ, Nat thought, hoping she hadn't broken the woman's neck as she rushed forward to check on her. A quick feel of her fluttering pulse and Nat knew she was alive, but things were not good. "Get a medic in here," Nat said without looking up. In response, she heard a team member speaking into his commlink while she continued to kneel at Jade's side. Suddenly, there was a scuffle behind her.

"Drop your weapon," the team's squad leader commanded as Nat turned to look. A situation was developing, one she should have predicted. Sal was in the corner, plasma gun in hand. The weapon was pointed at the ground but still presented a risk. The Space Rangers were only following protocol. With a last look at the still breathing Jade, Nat stood and paced forward as the Ranger repeated his warning. "Drop your weapon, or I will be forced to disarm you."

"You go ahead and try that," Sal replied, a coolness in her voice Nat knew all too well. The squad leader would be risking his life if he tried to take her weapon.

"Everybody, stand down," Nat said as she came up beside the squad leader. Before anyone made another move, the roar of a starship came from the windows. "What the hell—" Nat started but not wanting to take her eyes off of Sal and the Ranger.

"That's probably Cunningham escaping, actually," Sal said. "He was apparently smart enough to slip out the side door in the middle of all this mess."

Nat swore under her breath. This entire situation was going from bad to worse. Jade was hurt, possibly dying while she waited for a medic. Nat promised the director of the Space Rangers she would be capturing the dirty Chief of Staff to turn over to the authorities, using the evidence from the commlink recording, who, at this moment, was escaping.

"Don't worry, Captain," chimed in one of the Space Rangers in the squad. "We'll catch him."

Nat heard Sal snort a laugh and was not surprised. Petrus Cunningham would not be easy to track down. "You don't think the most powerful man in the 8th Galaxy might have an elaborate getaway plan?" Sal asked with a shake of her head. "Work it through, genius."

"Shut up," the squad leader shot back raising the barrel of his gun a little higher. "And I gave you an order to drop your weapon. You have until the count of three." Nat clenched her jaw. There was a decision to make. As the Ranger started to count and Nat watched Sal shift her weight to the balls of her feet in preparation to launch into an attack, she acted.

"Stop," she ordered stepping between them. It was risky, considering each was ready to shoot the other. "I need both of you to holster your weapons." When no one moved, Nat puffed out a frustrated breath, turning to Sal. "Holster it, Bransen. You can't win this."

For the first time, Nat saw a hint of naked emotion in Sal's eyes. Disappointment. Nat lifted her chin. She would not be swayed by the woman's reaction. There were some things which needed doing. Getting the business with Sal settled was one of them. "Holster it," Nat murmured, and Sal slowly did so. As soon as the weapon was out of her hand, the squad of Space Rangers swarmed past Nat and tackled Sal. The woman did not resist and in a second was face first on the rug. Turning her head to the side, she looked up at Nat.

"No hard feelings," Sal said. "I know this is simply who you are."

Nat nodded as she watched the men handcuff Sal. "I wish it could be another way," Nat replied. Sal turned her face away and did not bother to answer. In a minute, she was restrained and being lifted to her feet, as the medical team arrived. As two of the Space Rangers started to lead Sal away, Nat suddenly thought of Catherine. The woman was back at their apartment waiting for word. She wanted to come along, but Nat insisted she stay safe. For once, the young woman did not argue. *Because she trusts me to do the right thing*, Nat thought. *But what does that mean?*

Nat moved after Sal and the men taking her away. "Wait," she said, knowing in an instant the next sentence out of her mouth would change her future forever. Her career as a Space Ranger would end. Even though they would be able to clear their names, both from the recording, but no doubt from incriminating files Cunningham may have left behind, Sal and Nat would always be suspected of some involvement. Turning over Sal to take the blame was the only way Nat and Catherine would ever be entirely cleared, and she could possibly keep her career. *But can I look Catherine in the eye if I do that?* she wondered. *No.*

As the pair halted, Nat turned back to the squad leader. Putting on her most intimidating face, she leveled a hard look into his eyes. "These two rangers will stay here, and I'll take Bransen in," Nat said. "I want you and your team to keep this area secure. I'm not convinced Petrus Cunningham escaped and may try to come back in here to destroy documents."

"But—" the squad leader started. Nat held up a hand to stop him.

"You seem confused," she snapped. "I'm your superior officer, and you will do as I order. Now, dispatch your team to secure the perimeter, and I'll take care of Captain Bransen." The squad leader reacted to the tone precisely as she hoped, and as the man gave his men orders, Nat grabbed Sal by the arm and hurried her out of the office.

"What the hell are you doing?" Sal hissed as soon as they were out of earshot. "They will crucify you for this."

"Shut up," Nat said pushing the button to call the elevator. "Or I'm liable to change my mind. I'm doing this for Catherine, you know."

The doors opened, and Nat moved to go in, but Sal stood in place making Nat jerk to a stop. "All the more reason not to do this," Sal said. "Your career will be over. They might even arrest you if you don't take me in immediately."

Nat considered her words. She was telling the truth. Yet, a part of Nat was ready for a new chapter in her life. The Space Rangers were good to her, and she would forever be in their debt for making her the woman she was. She knew a part of her changed over the last six months. Loving Catherine, being banished to the training academy, even knowing Sal, all added up to a new way of looking at the world. She outgrew the rules and regulations of military life.

"I'll take that chance," Nat answered. "I need to hide you, until we can work out a deal with the Space Rangers. Now come on. I know Catherine is climbing the walls worried about us." After a pause, Sal nodded and got on the elevator.

"So, what are you going to do if you're not a Ranger?" Sal asked as Nat unlocked her restraints.

A glimmer of an idea popped into Nat's head. Something she fantasized about over the years while flying around alone in space during her ten years with the Space Rangers. "I have a plan. Once we clear this up and get off this planet, I have the perfect job for Salishan Bransen."

Clearly suspicious, but curious too, Sal lifted an eyebrow. "What's that?" she asked.

Nat patted her on the shoulder as they made their way out of the building. "We are going to go into business together," she said with a smirk. "To give you something to do."

Sal blinked at her. "Doing what exactly?" she asked.

"Recovery agents," Nat said. The more she said it, the more she like the sound. Plus, she somehow knew Catherine would love the idea.

"You mean bounty hunters?" Sal asked with a snort. "You and me?"

Nat nodded. "You and me," she said.

"Sure," Sal answered as the elevator doors opened and they walked into the lobby. "Why not?"

EPILOGUE
SAL

Even though Nat went against Space Ranger orders and stashed Sal in a crappy hotel room for a month, neither of them were arrested. Between Nat's contacts and Sal's extensive financial resources, things went surprisingly smooth. The charges against them were dropped once the details of the commlink recording and Cunningham's treason were revealed to the world. Jade Hamilton was arrested at the hospital for her attempt on Sal's life, only to later confess her part in the ploy to frame Sal. Sal's heroics in uncovering of the evidence helped her work a deal with the Space Rangers. Although she was no longer wanted for questioning, she was also forever unwelcomed by the Corps. Nat was also asked to retire quietly. She was "appreciated for her service, but no longer appeared to have the right code of ethics." In her heart, Nat agreed.

The plan to start a bounty hunter business stuck, especially when Catherine fell in love with the idea, and their friend Dee decided to retire from the Space Rangers as well to join their new enterprise. There was one moment during the business planning that was touch and go. In a meeting over drinks at the Sappho in the Sky bar, when Nat inquired about where all of Sal's credits came from, the group fell silent. Sal shrugged off the question. "Back pay," she said and was not about to explain the capital to fund their startup was from her countless space pirate stashes of credits. There was a long, tense moment between them as Sal watched Nat process this, but then the woman nodded, ordered another round of drinks, and never mentioned it again.

All of which led them to where the four stood on the sidewalk outside of a three-room suite in a business complex on the planet of Prospo. A NuForks artist was carefully stenciling words onto the glass door. His hands shook a little, and Sal was not surprised. Having three ex-Space Rangers and a beautiful woman staring over his shoulder to watch him work was undoubtedly uncomfortable. With a final stroke, he finished and stepped back. C & C Recovery Agents. One C for Sal's call sign of Chaos and one C for Nat's call sign of Catwoman. Chaos and Catwoman. *Incredible*, Sal thought still having trouble believing she agreed to go along with the idea. She felt Catherine take her arm to give it a squeeze. Nat was on the other side of the woman, wrapped in Catherine's other arm. "I love it," she said with a laugh. "You two are going to be an amazing team."

Sal raised her eyebrows. *Amazing something*, she thought, but let Catherine enjoy her moment. That was better than a lot of alternatives. If Sal had to admit it, she was in a happier place than she was for years. No longer hiding, no longer on the run. *Just a simple life for a change.*

Once the painter packed his stuff and was out of the way, Dee stepped forward and opened the door with a flourish. "Come on in, team," she said with a bow. "We are officially open for business." Sal shook her head at the ceremony but followed Catherine and Nat inside. The place was not too bad. Simple. When she first saw it a month ago, the area was sterile and nondescript. Since then, Catherine took over, and the walls were painted a calming light blue, a few potted plants were in the corners, and the furniture was professional, but comfortable looking. There was an office for Sal, one for Nat and Catherine to share, and a central area where Dee would run things as reception, dispatch, and the works. The best technology Sal's credits could buy outfitted the space. They were ready for business, although Sal was not sure how they were supposed to find people to hire them.

"I'm working on that, too," Catherine insisted. "I've placed a few ads on OogleGalaxynet. People in need will look there first." Sal was not so sure. In her experience, people in trouble looked in places less friendly than the yellow pages. Still, she would let Catherine run things her way. The woman was having the best time getting things started. *All in due time I guess*, Sal thought, about to tell the others she was going to go take a nap in her office, which she was smart enough to furnish with a very comfortable couch.

Before she could say a word, there was a timid knock on the front glass. The group turned to the door at once, all looking as surprised as Sal felt. A woman slowly pushed through the door. She was a petite red-head, dressed in an expensive pantsuit. Sal's first thought was she was a lawyer or something, and they were in trouble already. Sal also would have said the woman was pretty but for the deep lines of worry on her face. "Can I come in?" she asked with a slight quaver in her voice.

Catherine went to her taking her hands to lead her to one of the new chairs. "Of course. Please, sit down," she said. "What can we do for you?"

The woman responded by putting her face in her hands and sobbing. This was not what Sal signed up for, and she began to wonder if agreeing to Nat's idea was a mistake. She could be spending her fortune on the harem planet. Then, the woman looked up. Her tear stained face was full of misery, and she hitched in a ragged breath.

"I need your help," she said, and Sal waited for the next line, knowing things were about to get interesting. "My daughter is missing. I think she's been kidnapped."

THE END

Enjoy this book?
You can make a big difference

Honest reviews of my books help bring them to the atten-tion of other readers. If you've enjoyed this story, I would be very grateful if you could spend a couple minutes leaving a re-view (it can be as short as you like) on the book's Amazon page.

If you enjoyed KC Luck's *Save Her Heart*, read on for an excit-ing excerpt from

DARKNESS FALLS PREVIEW

I f the lights go out forever, can love survive?

When four women from different walks of life are brought together by fate to witness the end of the world as they know it, each must find a way to survive against the odds as well as learn to rely on each other.

Jackie Scott wields incredible influence as a magazine executive in Seattle. As she plans a smashing party for her fortieth birthday, everything is precisely as she wants it. But when a solar storm lights up the night sky in a dazzling display, it not only ruins the party but destroys power around the planet and Jackie must turn for help from the one woman she has tried so hard not to want ... Taylor.

Taylor Barnes is an Army veteran new to Seattle and wants nothing more than to find some peace and quiet working as a rent-a-cop in a corporate high-rise. When she is asked to attend the birthday party of the building's powerful and sexy CEO, she can hardly say no. Little did she realize every skill she ever learned would be put to the test to save the woman she can't seem to stop thinking about ... Jackie.

Anna Patten is a nurse practitioner who has returned one last time to the town she ran away from to pack up the house where she grew up. Trying to avoid any drama, she cannot get away fast enough, or so she tells herself while her heart wonders about her high school crush. When fate lands them together in Seattle at a birthday party, suddenly Anna must lean on the woman she once left behind Lexi.

Lexi Scott has built a simple life of writing novels and remodeling her farmhouse, but when she runs into a long-lost friend, her world is turned upside down. It's not until she attends her sister Jackie's birthday party that she is forced to not only face the apocalypse but now she must decide if she is willing to risk her heart again to save the only woman she ever loved ... Anna.

The end of the world is only the beginning.

CHAPTER 1

The attic was dusty and dark but for the single bulb hanging on a cord in the middle of the large space. Thankful she brought a flashlight, Anna Patten snapped it on and looked around. Years of keepsakes were piled everywhere. Boxes and furniture, clothes on racks, and old sporting equipment. *This is what happens when a house stays in a family for three generations,* she thought and started to work her way to the back of the at-tic. It seemed like a good enough place to start as any. Shining the light in her hand to the left and the right, she stopped when it fell on a box with her name written in marker on the side. *Keepsakes from my childhood?*

After Anna moved away and the house was empty, but for her parents, her mom had converted Anna's bedroom into a quilting room. Anna had never been sure what happened to her softball trophies or shelf after shelf of books. *Now I know,* she thought and set the flashlight on a table where it shone at the box. Opening it, Anna smiled as memories immediately began to wash over her. Her senior yearbook from Astoria High School was right on top, and Anna picked it up to flip through some of the pages. As if by fate, it opened to a photo of Anna and two of her closest friends joking around after a home football game. They were all decked out in purple and gold spirit wear, and Anna was even wearing a letterman's jacket. It belonged to the team's all-state running back, Mitch Wallace. *Now that brings back memories.* Their relationship had been complicated even by normal high school standards. Mitch was gay but afraid to death of anyone finding out. In a small town in Oregon in the 1980s, being a star athlete did not pair well with having an alternative lifestyle.

So Anna was his beard, so to speak, and she never minded. It kept all the other boys from trying to get in her pants. *And the ruse helped with other things too, Anna Patten, and you know it.*

Not wanting to think about all of those details right now, Anna flipped the page and scanned the other pictures. She realized she was in a lot of them. As senior class president and one of the top academic students, Anna remembered being extremely busy and it showed in how well she was represented in the annual. The hard work had paid off though, and she earned a full-ride scholarship to Stanford. *That opportunity to leave town and head out of state could not have come at a better time,* she thought. Her life in Astoria had become complicated and confusing. Thinking of it all now, Anna paused. A part of her wanted to flip to the autograph page at the back of the book, yet another part of her was uneasy. *Why is my heart beating faster while I consider this?* Feeling foolish for hesitating about something so silly, Anna defiantly turned to the last page of the yearbook. At first, she did not see the words she was looking for and then her eyes fell on them. In neat, clear script were five words and reading them now made Anna catch her breath.

WHENEVER YOU ARE READY,
LEXI

NOT MORE THAN FIVE miles away down a dirt country road, Lexi Scott walked with her two golden retrievers along the fence line of her twelve-acre property. Even though it was early, the sun was warm for an April morning. The tall grass was damp though and Lexi knew she would have to rub her two dogs down before she let them back in the old farmhouse she called home. As if wanting to let her know it was worth it, Rosy came bounding alongside her with a grin on her face. Her brother Clem was right behind her, and the two of them romped in a circle around Lexi. "What are you two crazies up to this morning?" Lexi asked them. Clem barked as if he could understand her and Lexi chuckled. "You don't say?" Picking up a stick from the grass, Lexi held it up for her two dogs to see and the animals immediately paused in their antics to focus on what their master was doing. "Sit," Lexi commanded, and both dogs obeyed instantly. "Now wait for it ... one, two, three!" Lexi threw the stick with all her might, and the dogs tore after it. The throw was a good one, and Lexi smiled. Even at forty-three, she knew her arm was still better than most.

When she was eighteen, the college recruiters had come knocking with softball scholarships, but she was not interested. To her, the game was a hobby, and so she settled for going to the local community college to take writing classes. In the end, the decision was the right one as her talent at creating imaginary worlds proved lucrative. Although she knew she would never be a Stephen King or a Nora Roberts, Lexi had a strong base of followers who always bought her books, and so she cranked out one or two a year in order to live very comfortably. It was with those funds she was able to buy the old Reynolds' place five years before and slowly fix it up. The project was a challenge from the start as Lexi knew little about remodeling, but it turned into a labor of love as she found joy and fulfillment in bringing the house and the land back to life. *Not to mention it was the distraction I needed at the time*, she thought with a heavy sigh. *I should never have gone to that damn high school reunion. It was dumb then, just like it is dumb thinking about it now.*

With a shake of her head to try and clear the unwelcome thoughts, Lexi started walking again and called to her dogs. Before the animals could get all the way back to her, Lexi's cell phone rang, and, grateful for the distraction, she answered. "This is Lexi," she said.

"Good morning, big sister," Lexi heard her sibling Jackie Scott say. "Out walking the fence line, I assume?" Lexi chuckled.

"You know it," she answered. "And let me guess. You're racing way too fast down the I-5 through the heart of Seattle because you're late for a meeting."

"Actually, I'm on the 405, but pretty much yes," Jackie said, and Lexi could tell she was smiling. "But I didn't call to chit chat about directions. I want to know if you're still coming up the weekend after next for my birthday."

"Wouldn't dare miss it," Lexi said, even though the last thing she wanted was to drive three hours into big city traffic. Still, this was a milestone birthday, and Lexi was pretty sure Jackie was not looking forward to it. *All the more reason to rub it in*, Lexi thought and grinned. "After all, you are turning the big four-oh," she said. There was a pause on the phone.

"You're loving this, aren't you?" Jackie said. Lexi laughed.

"More than you can imagine," she answered.

TAYLOR BARNES WAITED in the guard's booth at the end of the parking ramp and checked her Apple watch for the time.

She was happy to see Jackie Scott was due any minute and checked herself in the small mirror. Taylor knew she was being ridiculous carrying a crush on the classy but infinitely sexy CEO of Vibrant magazine, but the flirting was harmless, and the extra attention always made Jackie smile. As if on cue, the familiar red Audi R8 coupe came screeching around the corner and shot down the ramp. As it slowed for the gate, Taylor watched to see if the driver's side window would roll down. It was a cue Taylor had learned early on. If it went down, Jackie was in a good mood and would be willing to chat for a minute. Taylor was pleased to see the window dropping and stepped out of the booth. "Good morning, Ms. Scott," Taylor said as she leaned forward to look into the car and make a quick appraisal of Jackie's designer outfit. Taylor was indeed no expert, but if she had to guess the soft gray dress was expensive. *Considering how fantastic she looks in it, I'd say the money was well worth it*, Taylor thought.

"Good morning to you too, Taylor," Jackie said with a smile. "Are you working tomorrow?" Taylor lifted an eyebrow. Tomorrow was Saturday, and therefore she usually had it off. Although, other than spending the day at the gym and the evening with a good book, she had no plans.

"Depends on who is asking," she replied. Jackie tilted her head. It was a flirtatious move and Taylor wondered if Jackie knew she was doing it. *Probably not*, Taylor thought. Although Taylor had only been working as a guard for three months, she had yet to see Jackie with anyone, but her guess was the woman was straight. *Unfortunately.*

"Well, I'm asking," Jackie said. "I have a late afternoon meeting, so I'll need someone to let me into the garage." Taylor hesitated. As much as she found Jackie attractive, she was not someone's puppet either. Twenty years with the Army Military Police Corps taught her a lot of things, but a big one was to make decisions with your head and not your heart. *Or any other part of your body*, she thought. Still, Taylor knew she could get in a long workout in the morning and then come in to pick up a few extra hours. Although her retirement pay allowed her to live more than comfortably, there was never anything wrong with some extra pocket money.

"I can help you out," she finally answered. "What time?"

TO READ THE REST OF THE STORY
LOOK FOR "DARKNESS FALLS" BY KC LUCK

To receive updates on the status of all KC Luck books as well as get early sneak peeks and other fun stuff, please consider subscribing to my mailing list (http://eepurl.com/dx_iEf).

ABOUT THE AUTHOR

KC Luck is a bestselling indie author of multiple lesbian fiction novels to include *The Darkness Trilogy* and many short stories. Her books cross multiple genres and she has been an Amazon bestseller in lesbian romance, lesbian erotica, LGBT horror, LGBT science fiction, and LGBT action/adventure. She is currently working on a age-gap lesbian romance novel.

Regardless of plot, all of KC Luck's novels focus on strong female leads in loving lesbian relationships.

She currently lives in the Pacific Northwest of the United States with her beautiful wife and her six children (of the furry, four-legged variety).

To receive updates on KC Luck's books, please consider subscribing to her mailing list (http://eepurl.com/dx_iEf). Also, KC Luck is always thrilled to hear from readers (kc.luck.author@gmail.com)

To follow KC Luck, you can find her at:

Website – www.kc-luck.com
Facebook - https://www.facebook.com/kc.luckauthor.92/
Twitter - https://twitter.com/kc_luck_author
Instagram - https://www.instagram.com/kc_luckauthor/
Amazon Author Page -
https://www.amazon.com/KC-Luck/e/B07BK5ZRYT

Books by KC Luck

Rescue Her Heart
Save Her Heart

Welcome to Ruby's

Darkness Falls
Darkness Remains
Darkness United

Audiobooks
Darkness Falls
Darkness Remains

Short stories by KC
Luck The One
Naughty List

Made in the USA
Columbia, SC
01 June 2021

38844329R00155